On the Line

Robert Lecker

On the Line

Readings in the short fiction of Clark Blaise John Metcalf and Hugh Hood

ECW PRESS

CANADIAN CATALOGUING IN PUBLICATION DATA

Lecker, Robert, 1951-
On the line

ISBN 0-920802-31-1

1. Blaise, Clark, 1940-   — Criticism and interpretation. 2. Metcalf, John,
1938-   — Criticism and interpretation. 3. Hood, Hugh, 1928-   — Criticism and interpretation. I. Title.

PS8191.S5L23   C 813'.54   C82-094254-5
PR9192.5.L23

Printed and bound in Canada by the Porcupine's Quill, Inc. Typeset by
Debbie Burke. Designed by Glenn Goluska.

ECW PRESS
Stong College, York University
Downsview, Ontario M3J 1P3

This book has been published with the help of a grant from the Canadian
Federation for the Humanities, using funds provided by the Social Sciences
and Humanities Research Council of Canada, and with the assistance of a
grant from The Canada Council. The author would particularly like to
thank the University of Maine at Orono for its support in aid of research
connected with the preparation of this book.

Special thanks to the following people who offered valuable advice and
criticism: Russell Brown, Barry Cameron, W. H. New, Ellen Quigley,
Kent Thompson.

Contents

For Clara Thomas

Introduction

IN 1971 KENT THOMPSON published a survey of "The Canadian Short Story and the Little Magazines" in which he observed that "there is very little criticism of Canadian prose being written, and none whatever about the Canadian short story."[1] The absence of short story criticism persists today, despite the fact that many of Canada's best-known writers excel in the short story mode. One thinks immediately of Mavis Gallant, Dave Godfrey, Anne Hébert, Alice Munro, Leon Rooke, and Audrey Thomas; I think particularly of Clark Blaise, John Metcalf, and Hugh Hood. No books on these three authors' short fiction have appeared, and the few articles that have been published tend to obscure the originality of their subject by concentrating on thematic generalizations or regional emphases.

Regional and thematic emphases, of course, appear frequently in the study of Canadian literature; sometimes they are effective. But they have not illuminated the qualities which make our short story writers unique — perhaps because these writers are preoccupied, not with theme, but with form and technique. As David Kent has noted, rather than distinguish these writers by their attention to environment or idea, "it might be more pragmatic at present to distinguish our makers of short story by the formal attitudes they adopt to the genre itself."[2] John Metcalf seems to support Kent's view when he says, in a recent interview conducted jointly with Hugh Hood, that "The real problem is that people say, 'What is a book about?' when they should say, '*How* is it about?' They never look at the writing."[3]

This book originated in my attempt to redress the critical situation Metcalf describes. It was initially to be a broad study which, I hoped, would introduce and evaluate the range of formal attitudes comprising the contemporary Canadian short story. My goals were ambitious: I would provide some in-depth commentary on our most

important short story writers; I would refuse the obvious generalizations and concentrate on detail, metaphor, style. These aims were
soon shattered. The more I read, the more I realized that it was
impossible to write an "introduction" to the Canadian short story
which did justice to the range and complexity of our many challeng-
ing writers. Such a book might have been defensible in the 1960s; it
could not stand now.

How was I to proceed? I decided to concentrate on the three
Canadian short story writers whom I most admired. Better to deal
deeply with three than to present a superficial overview of thirty.
Clark Blaise, John Metcalf, and Hugh Hood are the most accomplished short story writers in Canada today. This study represents my
attempt to explain that personal evaluation — to myself and to my
readers.

Blaise, Metcalf, and Hood share many technical and stylistic
concerns; nevertheless, their writing differs substantially. Rather
than treat their work according to a pre-established critical or
cultural mould, I have allowed myself the freedom to respond
idiosyncratically and subjectively to these three authors. My
response is governed by each writer's aesthetic stance. I try to evoke
Blaise's tragic view of language, his absorption in the perpetual
struggle he sees between art and nature, savagery and intellect, his
sense of life as lie. The evolution of Metcalf's aesthetic is reflected in
the growth of his protagonists from boyhood, through adolescence,
to manhood; the three-part structure of my chapter shows how each
stage is identified by increasingly self-reflexive views of craftsmanship and written art. Hood's stories are so complex that I have
chosen to read one, and only one, that self-consciously explores and
interrogates the narrative act. The text of "Looking Down From
Above" is appended to my commentary; this may be of use to those
who wish to move from story to reading, and back. In short, I have
consciously avoided confining myself to a single methodology. My
commitment here is to the belief that the critic should not generalize,
that what we need in Canada is not classification, but identification
based on the distinguishing features of an individual author's work.
My attempt has not been to reduce the texts to an exegetical formula,
but to suggest how their profound, and very different use of metaphor, imagery, pattern, and language affects me. I want to "truly
apprehend" the stories as Clark Blaise tells us they might be
apprehended by an attentive reader:

When we truly *apprehend* something from a story, when, years after we've read it we are suddenly struck by the *appropriateness* of a word or an image or a character, it's often because we've gone beyond simple comprehension...well beyond anything deliberately in the story or consciously provided by the author. It is because we have finally grasped the *world* of the story and have found ourselves suddenly viewing the surface of the story from precisely the same angle as the author. And instead of a shimmering reflection — beautiful, undeniably — we've suddenly seen far below the surface. We see, in fact, that the story was only a single example of something much larger, more diffuse and practically unnamable.[4]

Since I am interested in capturing this unnamable, elusive quality, I have tried to avoid the critical frames through which Blaise, Metcalf, and Hood have been viewed. Indeed, in the Preface to the chapter on Hood, I suggest that Hood critics have become all too conscious of Hood criticism (amply represented in a very thorough bibliography by J. R. (Tim) Struthers).[5] Surprisingly little has been published on Blaise and Metcalf, I suspect because their work resists the kind of thematic analysis often applied to Canadian literature. One cannot discuss Blaise and Metcalf without commenting on their pre-occupation with form and voice. Critics have approached this pre-occupation in different ways. Barry Cameron's interpretation of five stories from Metcalf's *The Teeth of My Father* cannot be ignored; nor can his important reading of *Girl in Gingham*.[6] Together these pieces represent the most involved attempt to explain why Metcalf's writing is so effective. My reading of Blaise implicitly acknowledges the arguments of another critic — Frank Davey — with whose perspective I am obviously at odds. In the most influential article published on Blaise to date, Davey claims that "In none of Blaise's stories are there any overt uses of symbolism, metaphor, or non-factual imagery."[7] I want to suggest that Blaise searches rigorously for symbolism, metaphor, and non-factual imagery. He searches for these literary centres because in looking for his subject matter he is driven to a naked confrontation with art.

Critics may not agree on the impulses guiding these three writers, but they do agree on their importance. Blaise, Metcalf, and Hood are widely recognized as three of Canada's best writers. Clark Blaise, we learn, creates a web of "memory and desire" which "is so intricately woven that no single strand can lead us to the centre";[8] Metcalf's compressed narratives must be read, we are told, "with all the attention and effort that a good poem requires";[9] Hood has been described as "one of the five or six best short story writers now alive in the English-speaking world."[10] One of my aims in this book is to show how Hood has achieved this stature, how Metcalf's stylistic compression influences his choice of subject, and how the centre of Blaise's seductive web can be found.

Writers who share certain aesthetic principles are often associated with literary groups. For example, Canadian poetry has been influenced by the original contributors to *New Provinces*, by the *Preview* group, and, later, by the poetics of TISH. This kind of literary association is not prominent in Canadian fiction; after all, it was only in the late 1950s that Canadian novelists and short story writers began to openly discuss the critical implications of their craft. It is significant that Blaise, Metcalf, and Hood were the founding members of an important writers' group called The Montreal Storytellers.[11] Although their fictional subjects were dissimilar, the Storytellers found common ground in their belief that good writing should be both serious and capable of engaging popular audiences. The Storytellers' success indicates that their fiction affected more than academics: students would participate enthusiastically in the discussion following the Storytellers' well-attended school readings.

The group disbanded when Blaise moved to Toronto and Metcalf left for Delta, Ontario, but the desire to write formally accomplished, interesting fiction persisted. Hood had always been prolific. From 1970-80 he published eleven books, four of which were story collections. Metcalf and Blaise published three and two collections, respectively, during the 1970s; through the decade they also worked together as the editors of the influential series entitled *Best Canadian Short Stories*. The extent to which anthology editors are arbiters of taste will always be subject to dispute. It is clear, however, that by judging the "best" material submitted by hundreds of writers Blaise and Metcalf defined many of the standards by which good Canadian fiction in the 1970s was recognized.

Metcalf's impact as an editor and anthologizer of fiction can be compared to A. J. M. Smith's impact as an editor and anthologizer of poetry: both men have tried consciously to influence the literary values of a generation. Metcalf's sense of what constitutes serious short fiction lies behind the work published in such widely used anthologies as *Salutation* (1970), *Sixteen by Twelve* (1970), *Kalei-doscope* (1972), *The Speaking Earth* (1973), *Stories Plus* (1979), and *The Narrative Voice* (1972).

I mention *The Narrative Voice* last because it includes work by Blaise, Metcalf, and Hood, as well as theoretical statements by the authors which reiterate their concern with poetic form and texture. In an interview with Metcalf, Blaise defined "texture" as "detail arranged and selected and enhanced. It is the inclusion of detail from several planes of reference: dialogue, fantasy, direct passive observation ('I am a camera'), allusion, psychic wound, symbol, straight fact, etc. etc. —the sum of all that is *voice.*"[12]

Few will doubt that Hood's work is drawn from "several planes of reference." Indeed, Hood has encouraged us to adopt this view. *The Narrative Voice* includes what may be Hood's most important statement about his art. In "Sober Coloring: The Ontology of Super Realism,"[13] he tells us that he "turned out to be a moral realist" in his approach to fiction. At first glance a "moral realist" seems to be a writer who deals "with the affairs of credible characters in more or less credible situations." But Hood is never content to define a term or concept once. Soon he is equating moral realism with "Christian numerological symbolism," "practical stylistics," and the notion that "prose fiction might have an abstract element, a purely formal element, even though it continued to be strictly, morally, realistic." By the end of the essay, moral realism has been further aligned with "metaphysical thought," transcendentalism, "Romantic imaginative theory," "philosophical stance," "spousal union," and illumination by "Deity." "Sober Coloring" makes us more than conscious of its author's wide-ranging academic interests. Critics seem compelled to mention this essay in their analyses, and then to build on Hood's other self-reflective essays. This kind of dialogue between the writer and his critics has produced what by now is an established picture of Hood: a serious, intellectual, and complicated writer; a writer whose difficult, allegorically based work is infused with allusions to Wordsworth, Spenser, Dante, Keats, Joyce, Proust, Faulkner, and, of course, the Bible. Hood has demanded this view of his work. The result is that we no longer read Hood. We read what Hood and his critics say about Hood. In my analysis of "Looking Down From Above" I try to ignore the scholarship and to concentrate on reading the story without the aid of catch-words, jargon, or the typical intellectual biases usually applied to the study of Hood. Does Hood's fiction measure up if we ignore the critical contexts? I hope my reading proves that it does.

I hope it also proves that Metcalf's stories are, as Cameron says, an "approximation of poetry."[14] In "Soaping a Meditative Foot,"[15] the essay he includes in *The Narrative Voice*, Metcalf provides "Notes for a Young Writer" which emphasize his concern with stylistic compression and which stress his finicky attention to punctuation and form. He tells us (as well as his metaphorical "young writer") to "Avoid literary criticism which moves away from the word on the printed page and ascends to theories of God, Archetypes, Myth, Psyche, The Garden of Eden, The New Jerusalem, and Orgone Boxes. Stick to the study of the placement of commas." Like Hood, Metcalf stresses that the accomplished writer must "know the weight, colour, and texture of *things*"; and, like Blaise, he argues that "Stories, novels, and poems are neither idea or opinion. They are the distillation of experience."

It is no coincidence that in pursuing this "distillation of experience" all three authors present us with self-conscious narrators who confront their need to define and redefine the nature of perception. Metcalf's most effective narrators are accomplished artists intimately involved with the notion of craftsmanship; Hood's chatty mountain climber is, by his own admission, looking for "heightened perception"; and Blaise's narrators cannot resist the urge to treat the ugliest experience as the seed beneath their lyrical and frequently bizarre connections.

In *The Narrative Voice* Blaise reminds us, as did Metcalf, that "Fashionable criticism — much of it very intelligent — has emphasized the so-called 'apocalyptic impulse,' the desire of fiction to bring the house down." Blaise goes on to say that "it's easier to explain why things end than how they begin" because the beginning "is always a mystery."[16] What follows is an attempt to begin uncovering that mystery.

NOTES

[1] Kent Thompson, "The Canadian Short Story in English and the Little Magazines: 1971," *World Literature Written in English*, 2, No. 1 (April 1972), 17.

[2] John Metcalf, *The Whig-Standard Magazine* [Kingston], 16 Aug. 1980, p. 20.

14

3   David A. Kent, "Two Attitudes: Canadian Short Stories," *Essays on Canadian Writing*, No. 16 (Fall-Winter 1978-79), p. 169.
4   Clark Blaise, "Author's Commentary," in *Stories Plus*, ed. John Metcalf (Toronto: McGraw-Hill Ryerson, 1979), p. 27.
5   J. R. (Tim) Struthers, "A Bibliography of Works by and on Hugh Hood," *Essays on Canadian Writing*, Nos. 13-14 (Winter-Spring 1978-79), pp. 240-94.
6   See Barry Cameron, "Invention in *Girl in Gingham*," *The Fiddlehead*, No. 114 (Summer 1977), pp. 120-29; "An Approximation of Poetry: The Short Stories of John Metcalf," *Studies in Canadian Literature*, 2 (Winter 1977), 17-35.
7   Frank Davey, "Impressionable Realism: The Stories of Clark Blaise," *Open Letter*, 3rd Ser., No. 5 (1976), p. 65.
8   Michael E. Darling, "Of Time and Memory," *Essays on Canadian Writing*, No. 2 (Spring 1975), p. 56.
9   Cameron, "An Approximation of Poetry," p. 35.
10 John Mills, "On the Way Up," *Evidence*, No. 7 (Summer 1963), p. 107.
11 For a fuller discussion of The Montreal Storytellers see Douglas Rollins, "The Montreal Storytellers," *Journal of Canadian Fiction*, 1, No. 2 (Spring 1972), 5-6.
12 John Metcalf, "Interview: Clark Blaise," *Journal of Canadian Fiction*, 2, No. 4 (Fall 1973), 78.
13 Hugh Hood, "Sober Coloring: The Ontology of Super Realism," in *The Narrative Voice*, ed. John Metcalf (Toronto: McGraw-Hill Ryerson, 1972), pp. 95-101.
14 Cameron, "An Approximation of Poetry," p. 17.
15 John Metcalf, "Soaping a Meditative Foot," in *The Narrative Voice*, pp. 154-59.
16 Clark Blaise, "To Begin, To Begin," in *The Narrative Voice*, pp. 22-26.

Clark Blaise

Murals deep in nature

HOW DOES a Clark Blaise story *feel*? The tactile emphasis is crucial. Blaise's characters are inseparable from the things they touch — gooey, sticky, dirty, infested things that "ooze" through swamps, broken buildings, jungles. But if we read only for sensation (consider: "his brains are coming out of his mouth") or only for repugnant shock ("the hiss of a million maggots") the rawness metaphor seeps by us.[1]

Raw. The term obviously refers to the body ("bending low at the rear of the glistening carcass, the legs spread high and stubby, the butcher digs in his hands, ripping hard where the scrotum is"); but it is also one of the ways in which Blaise's characters live, one of the ways they know their world. Rawness lives with the primitive, "untamed" side of nature ("bloody scenes" and "wild cat beds" and fierce "unnameable fish"). Rawness takes you back in time to the amphibious and the deep ("nests of turtles and alligator eggs," "an ocean of alligators," a "sea of roaches," "sharks and monsters of the sea," "giant turtles snorting and grinding under my pillow"). Rawness (the "low brute force of nature") is anti-art. Savage and fecund, it beds down near "clusters of snakes" and awakens next to "copulating worms." The raw man is a nomad, a transient engulfed by transience. In time, in space, he wanders ("And then, knowing the role if not the words, I went upstairs to find out when we were leaving and where we would be going"). Raw knowledge: "life was unsafe." Raw action: "cavemen stoning a mammoth." Where? "Back in the swamps" full of "roaches and rats and lizards" that are appallingly present, as if they were being seen for the first time, elementally, in all their grotesque brilliance. Back to the raw beginning.

If you ask someone what they think a Clark Blaise story is about,

17

their first answer will probably not be: rawness. Critics have stressed the extraordinary sensitivity of Blaise's characters to "dilemmas caused by conflicting cultures" (Frank Davey[2]), their articulate response to particular "kinds of exile" (William H. New[3]), and their involvement with texture, voice, and "a creative ordering of events" (Michael E. Darling[4]). All of these descriptions are accurate. But the Blaise narrator is also defined by his tragic view of the social order, by the "sudden tragic nosedive" which disorients him and marks his plunge into a morass where spiritual and aesthetic values have been corroded or debased. No celebrations of life here ("I am death driven"); no celebrations of human purpose ("Nothing principled, nothing heroic, nothing even defiant"). Blaise's voice holds the tone of mourning: "Many things are gone for good"; "I who live in dreams have suffered something real"; "I felt a pity for us all that I had never felt before." The stories — elegies — return again and again to life tragically "crumbling into foolishness" and "darkest despair."

The striking feature of these lamentations? Their self-consciousness. Blaise's narrators are never content to live *in* their stories; they feel compelled to step back and suffer their commitment to these tales of pain, loss, failure. Still, they know that they *are* committed and want desperately for us to know that they know. They say listen: I will show you the face of loneliness in all its grieving detail, then I will tell you what you have seen. In another writer's hands this stance would have destroyed the integrity of the fiction by forcing the meaning into melodrama. But Blaise succeeds because he shows that self-conscious human intelligence *does* battle, *is* threatened at every turn. For Blaise's narrators, the ability to comment on art is an imaginative act achieved with great difficulty. To recognize the difficulty, remember the raw: primitive awareness ambushes Art; hurricanes blow away schools; bugs crawl out of rugs; homelessness assaults the meaning of maps, directions, roadways to the known; the inexplicable force of nature confronts the need for pattern, coherence, form. When we call the-world-made-into-Art "cooked" (completing the quasi-reference to Levi-Strauss) the consuming paradox of Blaise's fiction stands out more. The raw has to be cooked to be understood; but no sooner is experience digested than it is seen as debased *because* it has been digested. This raw/cooked tension informs many of Blaise's best stories. Reason tries to explain the inexplicable; the historian tries to order time which denies order; the educated imagination learns that man is a beast; the rooted teacher thinks about his rootlessness and finds that he is lost. Here we have the ironies stated in their broadest terms — terms which are uniquely permutated in the stories comprising Blaise's two books of short fiction, *A North American Education* and *Tribal Justice*.

The stories in *A North American Education* are divided into three groups organized around the experiences of three narrators. "The Montreal Stories" follow Norman Dyer, a displaced American academic who lives in Montreal. Obsessed with denying his roots, Dyer refuses to admit that like the Greeks and Italians he scorns, he, too, is a "new Canadian" foreigner. "The Keeler Stories" introduce Paul Keeler, another of Blaise's self-conscious, conscience-ridden characters whose travels force him to view everything as a reflection of his own tragic perspective. Frankie Thibidault of the book's last section is also a wanderer whose father (in the title story of the collection) pointedly articulates the two fundamental questions that Blaise returns to again and again: "You want books all the time? You want to *read* about it, or do you want to see it?"

Regardless of how they "want" It, Blaise's characters end up getting It both ways. They are educated to life through the books which prompt them to believe that experience can be explained, and observed; but what they see defies learning, assaults sensibility with the hard "facts of life," as Princess Hi-Yalla in "A North American Edcuation" makes clear. Education, as it turns out, means initiation into the body as well as the book. It means finding out about the physical as well as the abstract. The problem Blaise's characters face is that the reality they so painfully uncover destroys their inherent faith in the dignity of man and his creations. Without that dignity, why go on? One of the reasons people like Norman Dyer and Paul Keeler can't stop moving is that they are perpetually in search of an affirmation which can no longer be found. Or, as Blaise Pascal says in the epigraph which introduces "The Montreal Stories":

So we never live, but we hope to live; and, as we are always preparing to be happy, it is inevitable we should never be so.

There are, of course, endless ways of "preparing to be happy." In "A Class of New Canadians," Norman Dyer tries to prepare his own well-being by setting his education and "the authority of simple good taste" against "simple bad taste, wherever he encountered it." The contrast between bad taste and *bon goût* involves more than juxtaposing "the neon clutter of the sidestreets" and "Double-breasted chalk-striped suits"; it implies the cultural distinctions in which Dyer and his students are involved as well.

Dyer considers himself superior to the "new Canadians" he teaches though he, too, is a foreigner "proud of himself for having steered his life north." Rather than call himself an immigrant, he prefers "to think of himself as a semi-permanent, semi-political exile." He plays word games and loves the fact that he can play them as much as he loves himself: "*I love myself*, he thought with amazement even while conducting a drill on word order." Or again: "This is what mastery is like, he thought. Being superb in one's chosen field." Condescension is Dyer's true *metier*, and he never tires of reminding us that his teaching job, though "socially useful," was "beneath him." But the important point is this: without his teaching jobs (he holds a second one "to live this well and travel"), Dyer is nothing. Only when he is behind that podium is he differentiated from the masses he scorns. "He was a god two evenings a week, sometimes suffering and fatigued, but nevertheless an omniscient, benevolent god" who believed that in "teaching both his language and his literature in a foreign country" (note the wholly unexamined possessive tone) there was something "almost existential."

Almost racist might be a better term. We *can* condemn Norman for his intellectual bigotry, his snobbishness, his pompous self-indulgence. Yet, in the end, his delusions become pathetic as they are undercut by the "superb" irony of Norman's realization that Miguel Mayor ("the vain and impeccable Spaniard" in his class) is dressed in the "blue shirt and matching ascot-handkerchief" that Norman had studied with admiration in the window display of "Holt-Renfrew's exclusive men's shop." The teacher-Spaniard-mannequin equation is revealing: by implication, Norman Dyer is as vain and silly as Miguel, whom he describes as "a male model off a page of *Playboy*"; by implication, Dyer is as aimless as the "legless dummies" sporting the *au courant* ensembles which first caught his eye. Dyer may believe that he is cultured, that he knows himself, but Blaise suggests that we all sit with Norman in an uncertain class of new Canadians learning language from the start. Because there is no such thing as an "old Canadian," students of the country must identify themselves through American models, archetypes, dreams. In this context, the city is made only for freshmen, or as Miguel puts it: "It is just a place to land, no?"

Norman lands heavily in the next two stories in this section, heavily enough to warrant a revealing shift in point of view. "A Class of New Canadians" is told from a limited, third-person stance which suggests that the central character is disembodied, and, despite his ardent claims to the contrary, voiceless. Dyer arrives at first-person consciousness in "Words for the Winter" (language for a man who is cold), but the evolution from his idealism to hardened cynicism does not take place overnight. There is a transition stage, in "Eyes," during which the voice becomes more direct, yet still remains impersonal in its unusual "You" address, as if Dyer wants others to see the truth while he remains the fascinated voyeur watching bugs devour what he once saw as his bastion of good taste. By the time the "I" is in place, Dyer is ready to confess that things are not "superb." The dream shattered, Dyer admits that "reality hurts like nothing in this world." In the beginning, there is Norman, "Dishing it out suavely, even wittily. Being a legend." In the middle, things are less certain ("You jump into this business of a new country cautiously") and you realize that the moment before the Holt-Renfrew display has become the moment before the butcher's ("a Byzantine moment with blood and widows and sides of dripping beef"). Bloodiness replacing *bon goût*; fear replacing esoteric quotations from Faulkner. At the end, more basic perceptions of the community which was once seen as melting pot and cosmopolitan mecca: "We stand like cattle in a blizzard." "We are in the dentist's chair." And finally Norman tells us what he has denied all along: "I wanted to sink into the city," he says, "like any other immigrant and go straight to its core." No more "knitted sweaters, and fifty-dollar shoes," but "the purest cry of agony and sorrow I have ever heard." The pain. The rawness. "Reality hurts like nothing in this world."

In "Eyes" the raw core is still being held at a distance, so the speaker splits from his subject and becomes an other. One night ("in early October when your child is coughing badly") he is watching himself watch a panhandler watching his wife through a narrow slit in the "ill-fitting blinds." He considers the alternatives: "Do nothing," freeze the peeper in a photographic snap, or "tackle the man before he runs and smash his face into the bricks." Norman decides to do nothing (paralyzed by what he sees) because he recognizes that the voyeur is "a native of the place" and will undoubtedly vanish into "the fire escapes and alleys and roofs" he knows so well.

In one respect, the peeking panhandler represents the reality that

Norman tried so hard to ignore in "A Class of New Canadians." The true native is not the man who knows the bistros, the bookstores, and where to find the finest clothes; he is the man who stands faceless, a non-entity at the corner of the street. But, suddenly, Norman sees that he is no more faceless than the panhandler, that in fact *he* is that man at the window looking at himself, peeking cagily, furtively, at his life. Self-examination begins from outside looking in, so that the looking at the looker turns into a confession. Norman is finally able to articulate his foreignness, the distance between what he wants to be and what he knows he is. "And briefly" (don't look too long or too hard) "you remember yourself, an adolescent in another country slithering through the mosquito-ridden grassy fields" like a snake in search of sin. More "eyes" appear: the teenager waiting "in a motionless crouch for a myopic glimpse of a slender arm reaching from the dark to douse a light" (listen to the rhythms there). The panhandler has now assumed the form of Norman standing at the window of his past, and as the story develops, Norman's eyes move more: he is there, looking at "a movie at the corner cinema." He is there, staring at "the thud of fist on bone," or there, at the butcher shop, watching testicles snapped from scrotums, thinking about the calf's eye ("How you would like to lift one out, press its smoothness against your tongue, then crush it in your mouth"). Obviously the "eyes" of the title take many forms that go beyond the ocular. The central metaphor is perception, how we see through our senses, and how we digest what is seen, assimilate it to our own experience.

To examine the nature of perception is to view the "I" and all its positions in "this world you have made for yourself." But a story called "Eyes" that is narrated in the second person carries with it other questions, other implications that cannot be framed solely in terms of the narrator's awareness. "You" is clearly the reader as well as Norman Dyer. The relationship Blaise concentrates on is involved with reader/writer meetings. Reader as voyeur. Author as exhibitionist. The tantalizing movement of revealed and unrevealed. Things happening behind the blind. Narrative gesture transformed into erotic narrative performance. The window, frame, stage. Connections echoing enough to direct us to the fact that "Eyes" is emphatically about Art and the forms of vision it engenders. Watch Norman act out the role of artist as voyeur, moving from window to window in search of the most gratifying stance: "You move again," "you move," "you start to think of moving," "You're wandering happily, glad that you moved." The windows, of course, are implied, but are nevertheless very real.

Back to the butcher store. The man who wanders from street to street is the nomad in search of shelter; this man who wants to eat eyeballs identifies not only with vision (I want sight inside me, it is my food), but with the raw texture of the calf's "grainy ear." He hears beatings, fears his neighbours as primitive brutes who (in the blink of an eye) "would turn upon you" in a ritual of blood. Notice that the skinning scene caps the story, and, by doing so, points to Norman's transformation. At first, he almost believes that the culture he loves can still be found amidst the rootlessness which now surrounds him. "First you choose a place where English is spoken, with doctors and bus lines at hand." But as "Eyes" draws to a close he recognizes the primitivism of this "strange new land," and that recognition brings him to the sacrificial moment shared around the calf: "The women have gathered around the body; little pieces are offered to them from the head and entrails."

The body, bloodied, becomes the governing vision in "Words for the Winter," in which the calf of "Eyes" has taken on the larger proportions of the community caught, in the cold, like "cattle in a blizzard," animals surviving to be slaughtered after storm. After a first-person plural transition (self emerging slowly) the "I" appears, playing "the charade of ruddy good health up in the mountains north of Montreal." It's a charade because the narrator knows that he lacks the markings, scars, or stories identifying him as a true native of these lakes and woods ("too old," he thinks, "to ever learn the proper physical skills"). For Serge, a mystic who does know the waters, the cabin means vitality and resurrection ("'Three time already, I am a dead man'"); for Norman, it means the cliché of "sleeping in the cool mountain air from dark till the sunrise at 5 A.M." which allows him to say that "in this small way, I have succeeded."

But Norman's tone in the three opening paragraphs suggests that he has not succeeded at all. He sets up Serge as a model against which he is a failure and begins his narrative by announcing "the winding down." By the time we "drop" to the city in the story's second part, we realize that the facade of rural health will be buried in the "stagnant dome of dust and fumes" which "squats over the city." The images of declension assault Norman, swamp him in effluvia, make him realize that like everybody else, his sole aim is to "survive by subtraction" in this place where "winters are an agony." We are far from the Norman hurrying down Sherbrooke, stylish "collar turned against the snow." And we are far from the Holt-Renfrew mannequin in all its elegant pomposity. Now Norman has joined the bus lines of people he once disdained: "I stand with the Greeks and West Indians at the bus stop, wrapped in double gloves, double socks" trying to keep out the cold.

Think about what Norman is thinking about here. Not of William Faulkner, but that "your tongue could stick to those icy windows"; not of a good Italian restaurant, but of "cemeteries," "the dentist's chair," "nosebleeds," "much suffering," and "constant headaches." At first, you anaesthetize the raw wounds, novocaine the pain. But soon the freezing wears off. You lie there, naked in the chair, waiting for the drill to come. And when it's there, you retreat further, hide inside, only to find that the house you thought was safe (the mind you thought so stable) is a den of rodents, bugs, and sickness, with a "froth of mice" growing in a suitcase "as though it had an embolism," or roaches "staggering up the walls and falling back."

You begin to fight the savage war in earnest, get out the traps, the D.D.T., forget about language ("Best not to speak. Better indeed to kill"). And as you kill you know that something more than mice has died. "Dreams and failures" lie like corpses on the living room floor. Finally, you say it right out loud: "Something infinitely small but infinitely complicated has happened to our lives, and I don't know how to present it—in its smallness, in its complication—without breaking down." That's a crucial sentence because it isolates the paradoxical impulse behind Clark Blaise's fiction. On one hand, tragic recognition of change; on the other, recognition that the nature of change can never be precisely articulated. The inevitability of imprecision makes art seem a futile means of dealing with the tragedy it isolates. When they confront this futility, Blaise's characters don't give up; strangely enough, they make art through their destruction of all they once thought Art meant. So the teacher of "A Class of New Canadians" becomes the metaphoric wild man of "Words for Winter," defining himself and his milieu through raw rage. "I wished to annihilate them." "I was consumed with hatred," and a desire "to trample them." There is my son. I "shake him violently" until he is "white with terror." Not a very pleasant way of "preparing to be happy," to recall the Pascal epigraph.

Pascal's thoughts must have influenced Blaise profoundly, for he introduces "The Keeler Stories" with another quotation from *Pensées* which reminds us that "we dream of those times which are no more, and thoughtlessly overlook that which alone exists." Dissatisfied with the world around us, we search for escape routes from the present, but the harder we try, the more we find ourselves imprisoned. In one way or another, all the stories in this section of *A North American Education* are concerned with the effects of being locked in—to a building, to a fashion, to the doubts produced by knowledge, to a conception of existence which says: look, things are ugly and you will be framed by these things forever. Or, as Keeler says in "Extractions and Contractions," "everything will yield to roaches."

The title of "Extractions and Contractions" suggests that the twelve existential vignettes comprising the story will deal with different forms of death and birth. The extraction of Paul's tooth is part of the "long decline" into the grave; the contractions are in expectation of a baby which refuses to be born. Each vignette develops a central metaphor with which Paul identifies as he tries to understand his own shifting emotions. "Student Power," which finds the narrator trapped with others in a university elevator, is a surreal fiction about the effects of "winter's first seizure of claustrophobia." He imagines that soon the door will open and the occupants will all be "economically gunned down by a grinning student." Here the elevator assumes the form of a mass grave which implies that we are all condemned and "humiliated by overcrowding." The connection takes on more sinister proportions when we realize that the elevator is university owned.

"The Street" directs us to another version of extraction—the chill of Montreal in November, "The cold wind on a bad tooth" which "anticipates so much" and makes the narrator think of undertakers in white frocks: "Depressing to think the dentist, like winter, is waiting" for us to arrive, ready for the freezing. Bury the pain. Or remove it once and for all: "Quebec teeth are only replaced, never filled." What may pass for wit here is actually nervous gesture, the talk you make before something really bad is about to start. The drilling, "the platinum probe grinding in my cheekbone," "A nerve ripped from my body at thirty." And amidst all this gruesome pulling, the Blaise narrator *thinks*, can't stop himself from connecting images, extracting implications. There he is, "waiting for the freeze to take effect," wondering about the resemblance of this medical office building to a high school, linking the battle to save the tooth with John Wayne and "Incas performing brain surgery." Take the connections far enough and the tooth even gnaws at Jean-Paul Sartre. "When does it start—with a chipped tooth?" How does the "long decline" begin? "It begins in choices."

And what are the choices Paul has made, condemned as he is to be free? "There are days in November," he admits in "My Wife," when "I realize how little I've done to improve our lives, how thwarted my sense of style has become." Blaise's characters see thwarted style as the greatest (and most widespread) form of contemporary bad faith. We are condemned to thrive on the absolutely unoriginal and mundane, so the "afternoon gloom" seen "through the Fiberglas curtains is doubly desolate." Or, in looking in from outside, he thinks: "There is nothing distinctive about our place." How bored he is by pattern, knowing it so well. But to be condemned to pattern is to be condemned to life.

How break out then? How destroy the rhythmic structures, the insane regularity of the cycle? Perhaps through "The depth of my commitment—to trivia." Perhaps through the abnormal. Why think about the possibilities of bearing a mongoloid child? To be reassured that this complacent lifestyle cannot continue, or in Paul's words: "Because I seek punishment for the way we live...?" Yes, it is to seek punishment, purgation, absolution from our involvement in what is essentially a "low-grade art experience," *the* experience with which we must live, and from which Blaise draws astounding texture. But, in Blaise's hands, even low-grade experience cannot be left alone. The *degraded* essence must be wrung out, we must see debasement in all its putrid glory. So the sequence of sketches turns to accommodate the movement of descent announced by the falling elevator at the smug, but grave, start. We are heading downwards to "The Night," to "The time of the crack-up" when mounds of "gelatinous shit" cover the "Irish wool rug." Raw on cooked. What happens now is pure Clark Blaise. Paul heads into the kitchen, pulls out a knife, begins to scrape the dirt up, then to scrub the rug, and, all of a sudden (a truly unique fictional moment) he notices "glistening shapes staggering from the milky foam," black roaches "boiling" from the soapy water. Revel in the contrast between black and white. Watch the very brush that was meant to clean rise up with infestation, until it too glistens with waves of insects and becomes "the filthiest thing I've ever held."

Things turn against man, and the phenomenological assault splits all faith in the anthropomorphic impulse which once made place seem safe. It isn't that man finds himself stung into consciousness by *things* which gives Blaise's work its power, or even the fact that those things are so effectively scattered, like hidden mines, under a threatening narrative field; it is the *otherness* of Blaise's physical world, its overpowering, tyrranical silence, the brooding hostility which marks its brusque foreigness. The confrontation isn't with Nature, but with everything *out there*, with the world as it has been defined and structured by a human consciousness projecting its wants, fears, and delusions upon landscapes curdling against pattern.

You see the foreignness enveloping the voice in "Going to India," a story about Paul Keeler's visit to his wife's homeland. As the first paragraph makes clear, however, this is a metaphoric voyage, much more than a physical one. We will be reading a "horror story" about modern life, about the anxious moment before the plunge over Niagara which Paul shares with the newspaper's nameless Huckleberry Finn on his raft drifting over the unknown into the dark heart at the pit of the falls. Huckleberry Finn and Conrad's Kurtz: they come together, implicitly, in this modern voyage. Like the boy on the raft, Paul Keeler is wandering into a land of the unknown. And, ultimately, that unknown is death. So Keeler's flight (the metaphors keep piling) is inescapably metaphysical. It encapsulates and catapults a man's position in time and space ("Flights are a time of summary, an occasion for sweating palms. If I should die, what would I make of my life?"). But that is the question you're always asking yourself: it has nothing to do with this night, this flight alone. You've spent all your time telling us that you are a perpetual traveller; indeed, you've been anxious to define your writing as the poetic answer to insatiable physical movement, as if by writing it down you can prove that the plane can be stopped, that the boy will not plunge over the falls, that it is possible to make art operate against the "face of death" which obsesses you. As you say: "I started writing only of myself and these vivid moments in a confusing flux." True, the story traces Paul's "history" in thirteen unlucky parts, but do we really care whether "I was raised in Florida," whether he and his wife "were in Comparative Literature," or whether "My family is broad and fluid and...fabulously unsuccessful"? No. We keep reading because of the repugnant images which define this life in terms completely at odds with his defensive, self-conscious rationality: "I was slow, fat and asthmatic, prone to sunburn, hookworms, and chronic nosebleeds." "I" lived near "Jellyfish, sting rays, sand sharks, and tidal waves."

Knowing this past, knowing the prison of what Sartre would call Paul's facticity, we begin to read for what we don't know: why can Paul no longer come close "to saying that life was passionate and palpable and worth the pain and effort"? The answer involves more than identifying Keeler's gradual embellishment by *ennui*, or his vocabulary of *angst* ("dread and fear and suspicion," *"I'm not ready," "I'm not prepared"*). He senses so profoundly that the days when "Only living for the moment mattered" are long gone. The youthful, irresponsible, "hitchhiker over borders" has become that man who feels emotion "only in the face of death." *That* kind of emotion is eminently (fashionably?) existential. In keeping with the tradition of Dostoyevsky, Sartre, and Camus, Blaise ties Paul's anxiety to the recognition of social malaise. America is waiting for death, its short life "corrupted by wealth" and squandered in the pursuit of power. Hence "my belief that perfection could not be found in anything American." Squalid, backward India, "corrupted by poverty," rather than by wealth, offers a vision of hope *because* it is unknown.

What kind of hope? What redemption can possibly be found in this "receptacle of the world's grief" where, in a vivid moment of recognition, we see "a leprous stump, stuck in the middle of the flowers and fans"? Because Blaise's art thrives on the confrontation between sensibility and the inexplicable ugliness of the objective world, the journey into India becomes the art experience *par excellence*; it implies that the "visionary gleam" of which Paul speaks can still be found ("That visionary gleam; India may restore it, or destroy it completely"). But, even as he says this, the visionary gleam is being restored; after all, Paul is *writing*, defying the confusion he needs by patterning it into language.

The third Keeler story finds a younger Paul travelling to Cologne for what he imagines will be a romantic and somewhat Bohemian liaison with Janet Bunn. His visions of himself as "Viking in a yellow lifeboat," however, are quickly destroyed. Janet, he learns from a letter, has had "misgivings" and insists that "I must be free to act as though you weren't here." He meets Janet, but the tension doesn't abate, and they finally decide to get away, to visit Janet's friends in Sweden. For Paul, the Swedish experience represents a stage in his coming of age. Too typically, he sheds his inhibitions, frees himself from his delusions, and is left, at the end of the story, naked at the beach, turning "to face the sea." This is a conventional resolution to fictions of self discovery. Paul is a writer, but his work is too obviously about his own predicament. As Aino says, Paul's stories are like Chekhov's, because both men write "of humiliation." Yet it is difficult to believe in Aino's comparison: Paul is so conscious of his art here that his consciousness becomes an obstruction. He tells us in too many ways that "He was a writer, a creator; he would learn to satisfy himself with that." Paul never does learn to satisfy himself with life made into art, but he spends a lot of time trying, so the experiential structures seem forced, and the narrative voice sounds contrived.

It feels good to get away from Paul Keeler in the third person. He seemed much more genuine in "Going to India," when he was speaking for himself. By the end of "Continent of Strangers," however, we're ready for a change, want more of Blaise's sensuous style, more of the appalling contrast between acute perception of, and pathetic surrender to, a raw, exquisitely present landscape. "The Thibidault Stories" focus on this contrast as it affects Frankie Thibidault, who is seen as young boy, growing boy, fat boy, and adolescent moving from place to place over the years. Like Norman Dyer in "The Montreal Stories," Frankie is a perpetual traveller over borders, the sensitive observer who wants to be "creating the world afresh with his own pronunciations of impossible names." What is it, Frankie wonders, "What calamity made me a reader of back issues, defunct Atlases, and foreign grammars?" It was all the movement, "The loss, the loss," the "tragic nosedive" which, after so much defeat, made him "stumble back to Montreal a middle-class American from a broken home, after years of pointless suffering had promised so much." Clearly, Frankie Thibidault is destined to become Norman Dyer. And, like Norman who found roaches in his words for winter, Frankie finds that the life he wanted to make beautiful is infested with "roaches and rats and lizards," "footworms," and "chigger bites." This kind of infestation is symptomatic of a much larger problem infecting Frankie: to him the physical world is always threatening and on the attack. Refuge (he thinks) is to be found in history, geography, "with an ancient issue of *Collier's* or *National Geographic* taken from the pillars of bundled magazines in the attic," quick tricks with numbers and names; but reality (he knows) "is where eight people got killed in a head-on crash," where "the smell of furtiveness, rural slaughter and unquenchable famine" becomes a jolting stench, rank enough to wake up any dreamer. Especially Frankie. The stories in this section link his coming of age with the recognition of human failure and deceit, with an increasingly painful awakening to the fact that he is alone and always will be.

Yet it would be a mistake to treat such fictions as "The Bridge" or "The Salesman's Son Grows Older" in terms of conventional *rites de passage* patterns, for Blaise is primarily concerned with isolating the discrete instants of awareness which, in retrospect, give the maturation process meaning and form. It is in this context that Sartre's words provide an apt epigraph to "The Thibidault Stories": "Indeed it is not unusual for the memory to condense into a single mythic moment the contingencies and perpetual rebeginnings of an individual human history."

What is the mythic moment in "The Bridge"? Bridges have a way of appearing when some sort of initiation is at hand. As it happens, the "moment" in this instance confronts Frankie with the fact that his father is having an affair with Joan, the "unbearably voluptuous" secretary with a "harsh northern voice" and French-Canadian roots. But note that the discovery of this relationship, around which the story pivots, is never openly stated, although it is implied everywhere and finally grasped by Frankie in a semi-conscious moment which he envisions as the beginning of death. Viewed retrospectively, the discovery connects illegitimate sex and death, and it is the connection which bridges the story's three parts. Part one isolates Frankie's sexual awakening in curiously necrophilial terms ("I dug my well-scrubbed hands into the mannequins' dresses, over their cold unnippled breasts and up their fused and icy thighs"). Part two contains a much more direct brush with death as Frankie almost drowns (note the transition to French when Frankie's father wants things kept secret — *"Dites rien à maman"* — a transition reflected at the story's close when Joan talks of keeping secrets again — *"Mal si'l me voit"*). Part three finds Frankie out on his bike, "barefoot," and "feeling very Floridian and almost at home," when suddenly he is forced to make a quick stop that throws him to the scorching roadside. Frankie quickly discovers that he is not at home at all, that nobody cares whether he burns to death. But he discovers even more than this: the heat makes him delirious, provides him with vision that enables him to see the particularities of life on and beneath the river in a way he has never seen them before. And what does life resemble to this boy peering down through a knothole from the height of a bridge? It looks "like Coke at the bottom of a bottle." The comparison says a good deal about the carbonated, "bad for the teeth and stomach" lifestyle in which the Thibidault family is immersed, but that's not what makes the description interesting. Who will see Frankie on that bridge, looking through that knothole, and not recognize the voyeur from "Eyes"? There he is, peeping through a keyhole at the illegitimate, perverse truths which have shaped his life. The awakening on the bridge is as sexual as the passionate moment with the mannequins, and it is equally death-driven. Frankie "had the impression that I was going to die and that dying on the bridge... would be more pathetic than anything" (the word "pathetic" is his truest love). The bridge might kill him, but still he feels inclined towards "taking down my swimsuit and pissing through the knothole.... Maybe if I took off my pants and stood naked on the bridge someone would stop and give me water." It's difficult to ignore the exhibitionism here, or the nature of the impulse which prompts Frankie to think of urinating through the very peephole which shows him a winding-sheet of water, "a cool blanket to wrap my shoulders in." It's also difficult to ignore Frankie's embarrassment about his impulses, or as he says, "I was afraid of getting in trouble," or again, "People would know how I had felt." These feelings are clearly related to the story at large, which teaches Frankie two things that he consistently ignores: don't talk about death (it's a secret), and don't talk about sex (extramarital affairs should neither be seen nor heard, and if you ever feel the need to pee through knotholes make sure no one is looking).

There may be an element of humour in "The Bridge," but the story, like so many of Blaise's, is ultimately one of pain, confusion, and a burning sense of loss. In "The Salesman's Son Grows Older," the heat continues, "as hot and close as a faucet of sweat." The simile seems to be intentionally imprecise, as is the opening description of a "moon that burned hotly." I say "intentionally" because Frankie knows how to play with language. The distorted comparisons are his way of breaking free from pattern. It's almost as if he were saying: I can make the moon burn hotly even if it doesn't burn. I can control the cosmos. I can turn the night into a faucet, or roaches into "Camphor berries." All this magic originates from a narrator who is telling his story in retrospect and knows that the night will end with bad news. He doesn't plunge right in and tell us that his father was in "a pretty bad smash-up in Georgia about three days ago"; ever the artist, Frankie sets the stage, deliberately *introduces* the foreboding night, lingers over creating the "drowsy young patrolman with his tie loosened" who will (after a Coke is poured and iced tea served) deliver the critical facts. Control, control, control. At all costs Frankie aims for the control over *his* life story which will prove the look on his mother's face wrong, her smile ("not a happy one") that night which said, *"life is long and many things happen that we can't control and can't change and can't bring back."* Frankie's powerful recollections, however, say you *can* bring things back, can change them, can control life through art. Turn hot nights into faucets. Make moons molten. Blend roaches with camphor berries. Say: I am always moving but in memory I am still.

But not for long. You are smart enough to realize that it's all a charade. You look down at your sleeping son and there is evidence of your age. "Over his bed, five license plates are hung." His life decorated with the evidence of your travelling, your resignation and despair at what you failed to become. *You failed to live*. That's the story, isn't it? Or as you put it in words that amount to another confession: "Following the sun, the dollars, the peace-of-mind, we blind ourselves." *You* are blinded. And we follow you, in your story, as you move from Florida, to Saskatchewan, to Wisconsin, to Montreal. We watch you watching "the first time I'd ever seen a breast," or spitting out the clots of ink which summarize your schooling in Saskatoon. All the places are dead ends. The travelling has taken you nowhere. The metaphors you so cleverly juggled... even they may be meaningless shams. Is that why you give them up at the end, resigning yourself to the "shovel scraping a snowy walk" or to the "dusty rope" with its monotonous *"slap-slap"* in "a dusty yard, a little pit between the girls who turn it"? A little grave. A little execution.

Is there a way of rising above this depression? "A North American Education" is an impeccably bizarre tale of initiation which does end on an optimistic note: "What a day it was, what a once-in-a-lifetime day it was." To explain the roots of this optimism we have to understand the extraordinary feature of that day: Frankie is with his father.

Usually the man is on the road, or away, or emotionally absent in his drunkenness. But for this day of education, he is there, and, for all his failures, all his futile dreams, he remains Frankie's hero. Can you understand the boy without knowing the father? *"Thibidault et fils"* the picture says. The son following the father in a nomadic wake, changing faces with each new place: "Jean-Louis Thibidault, who became Gene and T. B. Doe." Doe the anonymous one. Devolution into facelessness. It's no coincidence that when Frankie begins to narrate "A North American Education" he is drawn to the pictures of his father's face, as if by resurrecting the photographs some starting point might be found, some identity picked out of the years to mark the story's start. The father is time. To find the father is not only to find your source; it is to find sources, a history, a context which will frame the restlessness, make sense of all the moving. In fact, isn't the whole story about starting points? You can't begin the fiction without them. So Frankie starts to tell us about his "once-in-a-lifetime day" by going backwards past his past to "my grandmother" and "my grandfather as someone special, a character from a well-packed novel who enters once and is never fully forgotten." This comparison is only half true. Boniface's visage was "both incidental and immortal." But how can you trace the Thibidault story if you deny the grandfather and "the face that could be dynastic"? And say you put your faith in the Thibidault dynasty only to discover that the patriarch is gone to be "a travelling salesman for Laverdure's Lawn Laddies," and that you are about to "begin my life as a salesman's son"? Well, there are two options: deny the dynasty entirely—claim that only the present exists—or make the present dynastic by turning it into myth. Blaise finds the first option unthinkable, so he resorts, reluctantly, to the second. Again and again he tries to find continuity, only to realize that the scattered incidents are all, that the writer has one chance to take a day and turn it into a kingdom: "What a once-in-a-lifetime day it was."

And we haven't even got to the raw centre yet, a fact which says something about the way a Clark Blaise story unfolds: first there is a profound confrontation with the narrator's relation to time and place, *then* the action begins, almost in afterthought, as if the real issue is not what happens but how the narrator asks himself this question: "what am I trying to comprehend in the act of telling this story?" Am I trying to comprehend "Sex," which, "despite my dreams of something better, something nobler, still smells of the circus tent, of something raw and murderous"? I keep my distance from the truth of Princess Hi-Yalla as long as I can, hold this

33

grotesque "dowager" at arm's length. But this show is *fascinating*; that woman is doing such strange things with her body ("The Princess inserted it slowly, as though it hurt, spreading her legs like the bow-legged rodeo clown I'd seen a few minutes earlier. Her lower mouth chewed, her abdomen heaved, and she doubled forward to watch her progress"). And just when I think I can handle *that*, this "big, sweating, red-cheeked" adolescent has an orgasm like an epileptic fit, right in the middle of us, screaming and all, and then a few minutes later *I* feel something "ripping at my crotch" and somehow I'm older than I was before and confused because my father is telling me to keep it a secret (I was "trying to cup the mess I had made") and saying *"I think there's something wrong with you."* My initiation day, "la déniasement," my first unsentimental education in "what it's like, about women."

Frankie spends the rest of the story enlarging his knowledge of "what it's like." He watches the women on the street, noting their "bra-less elasticized halters"; he steals "the early *Playboy* and its imitators"; he peeks at young wives who "hooked their thumbs under the knotted elastic halters" they wore. He watches all this and wonders how many others of his age might, with a touch more provocation, "plunge a knife sixty times into those bellies, just to run their fingers inside the shorts and peel the halter back, allowing the breasts to ooze aside." The "raw and murderous" education of the circus tent teaches sadomasochistic consciousness. And more: as in "The Bridge," where he fondled corpse-mannequin lovers, Frankie can't think of sex without thinking of death. From peeping at bras he graduates to peeping through the bathroom wall at the "voluptuous" Annette (note the similarities between this woman and Joan in "The Bridge"). And any old wall won't do. It has to be the bathroom wall. Think back to "Eyes," to "The Bridge," then return to this story. Why are so many of Blaise's characters voyeurs, watching from a distance, wanting sex, death, art? Psychologists would have a lengthy answer. Here is one that may be more direct: the Blaise voyeur creeps up to the window (the knothole, the hole in the wall — it doesn't matter) and what he sees is naked betrayal (the story in the other room — a tantalizing treat he can't have). "A North American Education" is about peephole teaching, and on the other side of the wall there is this truth: the things Frankie placed his faith in are corrupt. Annette is having an affair with his father. Joan is having an affair with his father. Norman Dyer's wife is cupping her breasts (for

34

the peering man outside?) "as she stands in the bathroom's light."

And yet...in the midst of all this "shame," this "complicity," this knowledge that "There was no place in the world for the life I wanted," still there is a myth which survives (is made to survive). The myth of father and son. Love's body. *"Thibidault et fils."* In a sense, everything before the last page of this story is nervous preparation for the articulation of this myth—the real narrative act. Put another way, the story *is* the last page, is a celebration of the "once-in-a-lifetime day" in the hurricane, "feeling brave and united in the face of the storm. My father and me." The rest of the narrative is foreplay compared to this. Frankie savouring the build-up to the last paragraph so ferociously brief, so holy that he is afraid to touch it. One day. One chance to get the story right. That last paragraph represents everything that is poetic about Blaise's art: the intense compression of language; the overpowering personal emotion implied in the detail of what is seen; the cadence of the sentences, their tonal wave from loneliness to excitement; and a concern with the sound of word combinations pressing on the ear: "safe from the paint-blasting sand," "flashing their foam like icebergs," "bellies blasted by the change," "glasses webbed with salt." Soon you begin to shiver, knowing what you've found.

Then shiver more in "Snow People," the novella which closes *A North American Education.* As in all of Blaise's most powerful works, the language here is full of shimmers, poignancy, fright. The linguistic combinations, while remaining accessible, consistently invite us to extend the implications of our reading until we are confronted with a nest of connotation. "Snow People" is told from a limited third-person perspective which focuses on Frankie's school days in Florida, and then on the inevitable travels which take him away from school to sit in motel rooms drawing pictures, getting fat, and wondering when all the moving will stop. But it never does stop. We are back to the Thibidault nomads, back to the jungle in search of food. The jungle, of course, is metaphoric. To the wanderer, new places are unknown, unsafe. Jungle consciousness is what attacks the Thibidaults in their search for a home. Jungle consciousness teaches Frankie a lesson, "a general principle" that he carries with him always: "something dreadful could suddenly cut him down without warning."

"So life was unsafe," and "he was" (he thinks) "the one who carried the scars." In fact, all the Thibidaults are marked by their flight into the jungle. It was as if there was "a rebellion of nature that only the boy and his parents were fleeing," fleeing to "more motels, rooms where the boy drew dinosaurs from memory, or rooms in the worst parts of the cold black cities where flecks of snow (at last) drifted against the black walls of tenements, like ashes from a distant fire." Modern jungles, modern caves at "the end of the world."

How survive? By inventing the world anew. By retreating into art. Frankie's vision of the world he can make by mind is his only defence against the primaeval panting at the doorstep, the frightening thing outside. On the one hand raw, "shredded" nature; on the other, built-up art. Disarray outside; order within. The dichotomies may seem blatant, but they take on more intricate meaning when we realize that the Blaise character is never satisfied to let his ordered creation rest. No sooner has he made the world than he feels compelled to break it down so that he can have a reason to build it up again. The tension between apocalypse and generation, holocaust and birth, obliteration and identity. Consider Frankie's words in "Snow People"'s quintessential Blaise passage:

> He looked out the windows, fed landladies' parakeets; drew maps of imaginary countries, harbors, rivers, coastlines, and lost himself in highway nets, urban sprawl, then named his cities in invented languages, devised their flags, labled [sic] the rivers and bays based on private words for water; watched them grow, and then with a cheap fountain pen dropped from a foot above, bombed them into rubble.

Faced with these deconstructions (and there are plenty of them in the story that have distinctly suicidal overtones) how is it possible to speak about character development? Better to speak of the break-down. "Snow People" appears as a collection of random incidents picked from a life which is random. Yet these stages in Frankie's life, displaced as they are, tell us much about the character of Clark Blaise's own tragic vision. Take the opening scene. By the end of the first sentence Frankie has been hit ("his nose smelling bone and all his side-vision gone"). By the end of the first paragraph he is remembering a brush with death. By the end of the first page a tone has been set: the story will gravitate to violence, lifelessness, and Blaise's sense of betrayal ("George Stewart had saved his life"... "now it was George...who had somehow killed him"). There is, of course, the Blaise counterforce to all this loss: Frankie's ability to stand back, even as he "pitched to one side," and consider his injury with rational *savoir-faire*. There he is vomiting, yet pausing to note "the yellow carton of Serutan on the toilet ledge" which "assured him that he was home" (only Clark Blaise would have caught this telling detail—the carton imprinted with "Natures" in anagram); pausing to choose toilet paper over towels because "Blood, his mother always said, left a permanent stain." And in the midst of all this "sweating and shivering," what does Frankie worry about? "He wondered if the blow on the head had made him a moron." Then he thinks of dying. The connection between stupidity and death is important: for Frankie, intelligence is life. But his tragic error is to assume that others share his view. So in the next episode Frankie is assaulted again because he has been stupid enough to let others know how smart he is. He had the nerve to be "an almost perfect reader who had polished off the year's book on the first night of classes," he was the odd one who "knew the capitals, all the capitals, and he knew the birds and fish of Florida." Still, there is one Blaise lesson he has yet to learn: his intelligence will always isolate him and make him a social outcast. And that is perhaps the fundamental paradox at the heart of all Blaise tragedies: to have education, sensitivity, and awareness is to experience pain, loneliness, and rejection. It shouldn't be that way. Always there is this sense of astonishment when the Blaise character realizes that his literacy has made him unhappy, this sense of frustration at the suspicion that perhaps ignorance *is* bliss.

Frankie is still in the process of learning, so he is willing to try again. But even before the confrontation with his teacher (a confrontation, it should be noted, which has its origins in the written word) he has begun to retreat into the "private travels" which find him "creating the world afresh with his own pronunciations of impossible names." Here again is Frankie the namer fated to be brutally unnamed. He steps to the front, begins to draw, and is rewarded with "five of the hardest" blows the teacher had ever administered. So much for being smart.

So much for being a linguistic exhibitionist as well, but Frankie still can't believe that people don't want the words he has to offer. So he tries, in another episode, to teach Broward "how to make figurines from plaster-of-paris and red rubber molds, the rudiments of reading, and how to speak." And once, just once, he has a chance to show off, to be a hero in his own eyes because he can speak French to the tourists from Quebec who consider him a miracle. The glory, like all the things Frankie wants, is inevitably destroyed by being publicly debased (what happens when the miracle of speaking is written down and published for the world to gawk at through hung over eyes?), and he discovers, once and for all, that "nothing secret and remote was ever lost in the world, was ever perfectly private" (I am condemned, eternally, to share my confessions with others).

If that's the case, then he will confess all: he is disillusioned with this place; he cannot understand why people's curiosity has died. He wants so much to prove that he can do something special. One day Frankie caught the ugliest thing he'd ever seen, a fish "with a blunt reptilian head." This, he thought, was "something that his father would want to see." Finally, he gets his father outside and there is this thing, "the same scummy black head, the mouth open enough to expose a set of nearly human teeth; the gills still heaving, but nearly all the body was gone." Devoured. His discovery has been devoured. Who will believe the story he will tell? Who will know that he really "had seen the worst thing in the world"?

One aspect of the fish story concerns the credibility of the creator, but the unnameable thing also says something about Frankie's world: it is disintegrating, being violently torn apart by inexplicable forces. The policemen who assault Gene Thibidault represent another version of this inexplicable force which wants to devour without saying why. Frankie's response is typical: "shaking in terror" he falls back on art, transforming the police attack into a western movie. "The Cavalry is coming, I can hear the bugles. They've got us surrounded, but we're holding out —."

Not for long. Soon the Thibidaults are back where they belong: in transit. And as they travel this time the road opens up to the end of the book, the end which Frankie sees through "smeared windows" of old hotels. The temptation is to say that for the Thibidaults nothing has changed, that there is no real end. The final sentence of the book announces only another move, another voyage nowhere. As Frankie anticipates: "... just as suddenly as they'd arrived, they were gone." What *has* changed, however, is Frankie's response to all this movement. Originally he delighted in new places and new names, never realizing that what he hated most was where he was ("Every name except the one they were living in filled him with wonder for the new things there were to learn"). Eventually, though, he sees that left in hotel room after hotel room, he has lost track of time, "not knowing the day of the week any more." What was once the symbol of movement has now become a prison: "He still wasn't allowed out in the daytime," and "A series of landladies" (kindly keepers) "would bring him breakfasts." And, like a prisoner who has reached the end of his rope, Frankie decides to hang himself. Of course he doesn't literally hang himself—but that is precisely the point: Frankie creates a surrogate Frankie, a dummy which "jerked and tightened and then swung back and forth, just so." All in good fun, Frankie might say, "hysterical" as he is with "suppressed laughter." But the swinging dummy sums up much of what *A North American Education* has taught: learning is deadly, creativity is suicidal, imagination is a prison difficult to escape. The story ends, appropriately for Blaise, on a note of absolute resignation. No redemption. No apocalypse. No sudden coming of age.

It is true that *A North American Education* traces sexual and social processes of initiation, but most of all it draws us into an aesthetic awakening. In one way or another all of Blaise's characters are marked by perceptual scars, lacerations made by the language they have condemned themselves to use. The narrators in *Tribal Justice* are also straining their eyes, not only by reading, but also by staring so intensely at their relationship to time and place. Again we find an emphasis on individual movement, rootlessness, the wanderer as hero, but the meaning of transience has become more personal. The stories in *Tribal Justice*'s three parts are narrated by deeply self-conscious men who make fictions about their self-consciousness. Although the narrators have different backgrounds and different names, their combined voices give the volume a rough sense of chronological structure in that the stories trace experiences progressing from youth to age. To concentrate on this progression, however, is to force upon the book precisely the temporal and spatial order which its narrators cannot find. Like the aborted structure of *Tribal Justice*, their lives are ultimately disconnected, yet they do all they can to convince themselves that *some* progression is there. The great deception afflicting Blaise's narrators is the belief that time and space can be controlled through art. But the movement in Blaise's stories is a metaphor of movement without centre. All the attempts to recollect, to put the past in perspective, imply that the world has lost touch with its origins, and Blaise wonders: how can society know itself without knowing its history? How can you figure out where you are if you don't know where you've been?

Some will say that these are old, old questions, and Blaise, I think, would agree, might even say that they are the only questions worth addressing again and again. A Clark Blaise story is always marked by the presence of a narrator who, in one way or another, is trying to enter history and understand how it has affected him. And the consistent conflict is this: the narrator who thirsts for continuum knows that he will never have it; the narrator who wants continuity and the world will have to be satisfied with a motel room, a trailer, a car. What do you do when you can't recapture worlds, generations, histories of the tribe? You resort to metaphor and see the universe in what's at hand. So the tribe in the book's title does not only mean family and heritage; it refers to all societies and the rituals which make them cohere and incohere. In *Tribal Justice*, Blaise concentrates again on the North-American tribe and on the primitive impulses directing a society which thinks that it lives by reasonable rules called "justice," when in fact "justice" means retribution or irrational attack. The irony is obvious: the tribe is contemporary life; its justice is the crime it perpetrates by alienating those who are different, by displacing those who evade the fortress of communal identity. And who are "those"? Clark Blaise's French Canadians, blacks, Jews. Clark Blaise's narrators, who all sense that what everybody calls civilized is actually crude and primitive. Clark Blaise's outcasts, who cook experience (make it just so) while everybody else is scavenging for animal shreds (hungry, ready to eat anything, no matter how it comes).

Tribal Justice yokes two warring worlds: one world holds within it swamps, alligators, hurricanes, crudity, poverty, filth, aggression; the other tries to hold within it history, golden cities, timeless patterns, essence of things, the conviction that man can civilize the tribe and record its unspoken rules. The first story, "Broward Dowdy," is framed by a very concrete war. The narrator tells us that the year is 1942, that "my father was drafted," and that he and his mother had started to travel in search of work. Although the narrator's memory of his father is as "blurred" as his understanding of the showdown in "the Pacific Theater," the war affects him profoundly, despite his (ironic) claim that his summer with Broward "was an idyl." The truth is that he cannot see his daily experiences as anything less than a threatening, para-military operation, expeditions into jungles which are unknown, unsafe. So "the fishing every day with

Broward became in my imagination something of a tactical maneuver." Now it is possible to read "Broward Dowdy" as a record of the first of many tribal markings the narrator will come to bear. But in what sense do we remember this initiation after the book is closed? We don't remember it as a story about Broward Dowdy, but as the narrator's shocked realization that Broward Dowdy's family story may in fact be true to life. We remember it as the process by which the narrator learns that everything is violent, that things are infested and falling apart, that everybody is moving without any end in sight.

Everything is violent. Broward takes a turtle and "slammed it furiously to the floor, as though it were a tiny coconut, then fired it against the wall until at last, mercifully, the bottom shell snapped off" (note the military language here: later the narrator will see a deceiving picture of his father, "holding a coconut in his hand and grinning just like he did at home"). Soon the narrator becomes more articulate about the nature of the battle he is fighting in these Florida swamps: "...I reconstructed assaults and casualties. Turtles became tanks,...and the endless wriggling hordes of bream were Japs and their numbers hacked with glee."

Things are infested and falling apart. "The bulging bottom was gnawed open and here and there lay conical deposits, like anthills." "Even the swarm of fruit flies buzzing around the mounds of lavender-crusted oranges were anxious to escape." The images, of course, are particular to "Broward Dowdy," but they also remind us of the roaches in "Words for the Winter," the hookworms in "Going to India," or "the hiss of a million maggots" in "The Salesman's Son Grows Older." And, as in the other stories, the buzzing, gnawing, hissing, and devouring point beyond one setting to a saprogenic universe seen in "an almost nauseating vision," or through a "face of flies."

How can this rawness be countered? If the Blaise character can find something to believe in—any evidence of human nobility transcending savage impulse—he holds on to it as long as he can. Broward, patient with his family and consistently polite, is noble enough to become the putative basis for the story and its title. "Putative" because Broward (whose body is revealingly "pale and brilliant" in contrast with "the sour muck" that surrounds him) is ultimately not the centre: Blaise focuses on the loss felt by a narrator who knows that Broward will soon be gone, who knows that Broward will only last a summer.

For Clark Blaise, for the story, we come back to this truth: everybody is moving without any end in sight. Consider this statement in the context of "Broward Dowdy"'s first paragraph. The essence of the story — its central preoccupation with displacement and temporal jitteriness — is captured there in fourteen lines. We meet the narrator as a nomad once again. He moves three times from town to town, and these shifts are reflected in language full of references to change: "we were living," "shortly," "for a month," "passed on," "immediately," "within a couple of days," "now," "moving North." This kaleidoscopic temporal and spatial introduction says much about its teller: he is as unstable as his style. And the first sentence suggests the chief cause of this instability: "my father was drafted." Drafted — the word embodies the sense of separation and loss which drives the narrator on in his aimless attempt to reconstruct his drafted roots. But the word also points to the overpowering impact of war on the speaker and those around him. It is the war which has unhoused the narrator, his mother, "an old high school friend" (also "drafted"), the "Wisconsin woman," and "a watermelon farmer" who has gone North "to work in a factory." As the farmer's pilgrimage suggests, these people are controlled by the availability of jobs. Slaves to seasonal employers, they have become the prey of regional industry as well. At the end of the story we find the Dowdys, like the farmer, assuming this role of prey as they prepare "to leave the summer moss-picking grounds and head back up to the pecanfields of Georgia." Nothing has stabilized, and the implication of the first paragraph never abates. At the end, plans are being made for the soldier's (salesman's) family to make another move: "we were to be resettled in South Carolina in special quarters for servicemen's dependents."

In "Relief," what appears to be the same family has been re-united and returned to Florida, where we find them living near Lake Oshacola. The narrator, now called Lester, is older, and he is beginning to explain the landscape in more precise terms. Lester clearly divides his world between two views. There is the hurricane at the doorstep, or the promontory in the swamps where he lives, "untamed," with "pumas" and "wildcats that shredded your wash." Away from this peninsula, however, life is more civilized. Technology warns of storms ("Those with radios were safe from hurricanes, in their snug bungalows on landscaped streets"), and Miss Hewitt tries to teach the swampdwellers about sanitation, equality, and charity.

But this attempt to tame the jungle never works; it only makes the distinctions between raw and cooked consciousness that much clearer. Half of Lester responds to his teachers out of the classroom. His father knows that "it was fixing to storm bad with all this moisture in the air." He doesn't need the radio. And neither does Leon Sellers when he tells Lester about changes in the water level at the lake. But Lester's school-bred half contradicts what deceivingly appears to be the story's central point: that you shouldn't talk about hurricanes unless you've been in one. Does Lester really believe that you have to be frozen in fright next to churning gators before you can write about them? Or would he say that the real "relief" in the story is provided by his imagination, that the narrative process can transform any experience at the drop of a word? Remember Lester in school the day before the storm. "My reading assignments that morning had concerned a frontier family cut off by a blizzard and their near-starvation before relief had come." That is the story's key sentence; in fact, it is the sentence propelling all of Lester's narrative, which transforms the frontier family's near-death in a blizzard into Lester's (frontier) family's mock near-death in a hurricane. In other words, Lester has been involved with the experience of *narrating* the hurricane, and turning it into art. His story is about the images and metaphors you use when you want to tell the story of a hurricane. The school-room reading is about the fiction of what it means to write a story about a hurricane. Relief: it's not really true. The fiction saves me. It is because "Relief" is about the dream of a hurricane, rather than the hurricane story itself, that we are not drawn into the ostensible moral issues which are presented. Instead, we keep coming back to the raw/cooked tension as it gives shape to a *manner* of telling, to a knowledge of the ingredients from which the telling act is composed.

"The Fabulous Eddie Brewster" is also set in Florida. Unlike "Relief" and "Broward Dowdy," however, this story ironically plays out the great American dream of plenty through Etienne, a displaced Canadian who moves from rags to riches to political power in the brief space of a decade following World War II. Unfortunately, neither Etienne's history in France, nor the changes he undergoes in America, are interesting. The character is there as proof of Blaise's conviction that the minority member often becomes "fabulous" by selling short his cultural roots. When Frankie's mother notes that Etienne's French cooking "reminds me of Montreal," the comment "soured him; one thing he resented was those remote origins." Etienne would rather be Eddie. The Rustique restaurant he establishes, replete with its dancers from Cuba ("since they're cheap") makes a mockery of his French connection and shows him to be much more at home in the manipulative American style which he thrives on with a flurry. Or as Frankie's mother puts it after he has announced that "I'm going into business": "Etienne—what an American you are." Eddie *is* the archetypal, born-again entrepreneur, the salesman *par excellence* ironically exploiting his own French roots to make himself "one of the richest men in the country." The truth, of course, is that Frankie sees Eddie as the unique embodiment of the myth of American well-being, when in fact his uncle becomes just another middle-class businessman getting fat, playing golf, huffing up the stairs. We soon understand that the title of the story is to be spoken with tongue in cheek. Eddie is not fabulous, but faceless. His wealth is founded on his willingness to abandon his heritage—the tribe—in favour of affluent pseudo-fame.

Yet Etienne is not the only person to shortchange his tribe. Lou has also sought out the American dream. The States, "he surmised," was where "a fortune waited," and he was convinced that "the future flow of money was southward." He accuses native French Canadians of being "afraid to leave Quebec." They were "Just *habitants* by his standards, whose children would be raised on beans and black bread for Sunday breakfast." Lou makes a bit more money in Florida than he did in Montreal, but he soon finds that "Florida had not been the gold mine he'd hoped for." Still, he keeps looking for the ultimate get-rich-quick-plan, never pausing to realize that he is married to his dream of Mammon, rather than to Mildred. The last sentence of the story confirms Frankie's parents' inevitable divorce and suggests that the entire story be seen as the record of cultural and linguistic divorce as well—a breakup which takes on larger meaning in its relation to the American dream gone bad. The pursuit of wealth divides the family, disrupts the tribe, and removes the value of heritage to make room for the all-powerful buck. This message may be too clear. Although the story centres on one of Blaise's most prominent themes —the relationship between displacement and morality—it lacks a strong, involved narrative voice and the richness of detail that Blaise is capable of achieving through first-person point of view. Where is Frankie Brossard? Where is the voice that mocks its own presentation of the Eddie Brewster myth? We find it again in "Grids and

Doglegs," one of Blaise's most successful, and self-consciously bizarre stories.

Blaise has said that in an effective short story ". . . the first paragraph is a microcosm of the whole, but in a way that only the whole can reveal."[5] Judged by this standard, "Grids and Doglegs" is an exceptionally effective piece whose first paragraph captures some definitive Blaise tensions:

> When I was sixteen I could spend whole evenings with a straightedge, a pencil, and a few sheets of unlined construction paper, and with those tools I would lay out imaginary cities along twisting rivers or ragged coastlines. Centuries of expansion and division, terrors of fire and renewal, recorded in the primitive fiction of gaps and clusters, grids and doglegs. My cities were tangles; inevitably, like Pittsburgh. And as I built my cities, I'd keep the Pirates game on (in another notebook I kept running accounts of my team's declining fortune... "Well, Tony Bartirome, that knocks you down to .188 . . ." the pre-game averages were never exact enough for me), and during the summers I excavated for the Department of Man, Carnegie Museum. Twice a week during the winter I visited the Casino Burlesque (this a winter pleasure, to counter the loss of base-ball). I was a painter too, of sweeping subjects: my paleobotan-ical murals for the Devonian Fishes Hall are still a model for younger painter-excavators. (Are there others, still, like me, in Pittsburgh? This story is for them.) On Saturdays I lectured to the Junior Amateur Archaeologists and Anthropologists of Western Pennsylvania. I was a high school junior, my parents worked at their new store, and I was, obviously, mostly alone. In the afternoons, winter and summer, I picked up dirty clothes for my father's laundry.

The narrator can't wait to tell us about time, space, and art. Look at him, in the very first sentence, brandishing the "tools" which allow him to create "cities" in an evening, to envision "Centuries" on a page, to rule the whole world with a "straightedge" wielded for control. But then there is the raw edge along which the cities are placed—"ragged coastlines" of "twisting rivers" which resist the ruler's line. Now history begins to run in reverse: we move through "Centuries of expansion" back to barbarian battle; simultaneously,

45

we move forward, like the phoenix, from "fire" to "renewal," until
the primitive "terrors" have been shaped, gridded into form. Still,
the raggedness survives this ferocious building. "My cities were
tangles" as much as jungles, or treacherous seas where all was
unsafe. It's no accident that the story begins in Pittsburgh (city of
steel) where the narrator watches the Pirates on TV (plunderers from
the past dressed for the global village). They play; he calculates
averages. They perform the ritual; he watches the ritual performed.

Here is this guy who starts his story by talking about a pencil. Four
sentences later he's telling us about his excavation work for the
"Department of Man, Carnegie Museum" (digging up the past,
humanizing the present, archaeological impulse confirmed). Only
Clark Blaise would give us the Museum (not only the Museum, mind
you, but the Department of *Man*) in the same sentence as the Pirates'
game and records of "my team's declining fortune." The emphasis on
declension is by no means gratuitous. The team is failing, and, as we
follow it, our gaze inevitably (metaphorically) travels down. So we
naturally arrive at "excavated." Something primitive, submerged, is
going to be revealed. We are going *to go under* and unearth the past,
burrowing beneath cities into unimaginable prehistoric truth. The
archaeological epiphany sprung from fossilized bone. But consider
that word again: "excavated." The *art* of digging, *the dig*. The
reconstruction. Gluing back the bones. Making the shape — again.
Finding the pattern — again. The excavation is about artistic choices.
"Casino Burlesque" on the one hand, "Carnegie Museum" murals
on the other. Blaise wants to stress the interdependence of primitivism and ratiocination, the raw/cooked juncture. So the boy who
watches baseball and burlesque soon articulates the role he has
suggested all along: "I was a painter too. . . ." Yes, but *what* does he
paint? "Paleobotanical murals" are the obvious choice. His art is
apt, for it encompasses ancient (*palaios*) and present (the murals are
"*still* a model" [emphasis added]). Note the two-sided term by
which he refers to the "younger painter-excavators" who have
followed in his footsteps. And listen to the way he finally *calls*
himself a painter, smirking with satisfaction at the intricacy of image
masked by supple, deceptively casual prose. There are three final
sentences. The first says I AM SMART, "I lectured to the Junior
Amateur Archaeologists" (Blaise's narrators like to tell us about their
I.Q.). Then a transition: "I was a high school junior" (I was not so
smart, I lived on dreams and was "mostly alone"). To the deflated

close: "I picked up dirty clothes for my father's laundry" (back to rawness, handling dirt).

The paragraph provides a curious introduction to a story tracing Norman Dyer's "high school years." What does all this *talk* about paper, baseball, and excavation have to do with the Women's Club College Prom? Everything, because the central event (what *happens* in a Clark Blaise story) is verbal (the plot is about language, the dance of words, the tonal turns). The chief subject of "Grids and Doglegs" is not the Prom, or Cyndy Godwin, or Buhl Planetarium, it is the *way* Norman speaks about these things. One part of Norman Dyer (the "certifiably brilliant" part) loves to philosophize, to describe life with cool cynicism and ironic detachment (examine the voice which parenthetically qualifies experience throughout the story). There he is, telling us that "Compared to the vacant dimensions of space—of time, distance, and temperature—what could be felt for Eisenhower's heart attack, Grecian urns, six million Jews, my waddle and shiny gabardines?" In a single sentence: the universe, the president, Keats, truth, beauty, the holocaust, history, and *gabardines*. Norman says that the things that "mattered" were "large, remote and perpetual," but he can't stop talking about his fascination with things like gabardines.

This fascination reveals an aspect of his personality completely at odds with the sophisticated, chess-playing, "self-respecting intellectual." We hear *Norman* as well as *Normie*. Normie is the adolescent who spends a night "to learn the Lord's Prayer backwards," who talks about snapping bra straps and impressing his date with *filet mignon*. What makes the story interesting is that retrospective Norman can't stop telling us that Normie's existence is a cliché—the line practised "a hundred times" only to be "badly acted"; the headlights "slapped" ("hoping they would shatter and I could bleed to death"). Norman is obsessed with Normie's artifice. Why pretend that you can say something new? After all, the "certifiably brilliant" know that everything has been said before. This is the knowledge that makes Norman's narrative strange. No sooner has he said something than he stands back and tries to tell us how crude his creation is, how absolutely unoriginal his perceptions are: "Nothing matters, except, perhaps, the proper irony. I had that irony once (I wish, in fact, I had it now)." The art in the story, we begin to realize, is about the making of art. Dramas keep coming up in Norman's head (note the repeated allusions to the stage): Play one: Normie creating cities; Play two: Normie painting; Play three: Normie playing chess with Keith Godwin; Play four: Normie grinding out a lens; Play five: Normie saying "Om" in school; Play six: Normie at the prom. And on and on. All those masks, outfits, makeup, roles ("she wore glittering earrings and a pale sophisticated lipstick that made her lips look chapped"). Norman spends his time painting these scenes, masking the faces. But the moment the mask is finished he wants to rip it off, knowing that the play has not caught reality, that the art is a lie (compare, for example, the imagined doglegged streets of the opening with the much baser dogleg implied at the story's end: "There's a hydrant up there. Why don't you use it"). The great unmasking of raw truth reveals...only another mask to be destroyed. Like Norman, Blaise won't let things rest. He's never satisfied until we learn that what we thought was beautiful is in fact a sham. The story exists, like the "humiliating science" of astronomy, as "a destroyer of pride in human achievement, or shame in human failings." In this sense, it comments on more than Norman Dyer and his high school days. The astronomy and archaeology metaphors tell us that the folly-ridden subject is man, whose passions bind him to pettiness and pride.

"I'm Dreaming of Rocket Richard" is told by a less sophisticated narrator than Norman Dyer, but this French Canadian, nicknamed "Curette" in his childhood, is acutely conscious of the "human failings" which allowed his father to be humiliated and finally "squashed like a worm underfoot." The story is about dreams — of "gods on the ice" and "the intimacy of old-time hockey," of a right "to the world in the *Gazette* and on the other side of Atwater," of the hope "that a little initiative and optimism would carry us anywhere but deeper into debt and darkest despair." But the dreams are all crushed. Here, as in so many of Blaise's stories, the narrator learns that he is an outcast without a true home, the offspring of a man whose destiny was to be "told off, turned down, laughed at."

On its surface, the story follows the family in its journey to visit the Schmitzes, relatives from New Hampshire who have moved to Florida and set up a chain of dry cleaning stores. The narrator's father "expected to become the manager of a Schmitz Dry Kleenery." Of course he fails. Brother-in-law Schmitz isn't interested in a man who drinks too much, can't speak the language, and can't dress the part. The family returns to Montreal, and the narrator knows that "we'd hit the bottom." He knew this from the start. But we follow his recollections because they reveal the son's own failure to cope with the clash of American and Canadian cultures, and his desperate attempt to find an impossible harmony between two worlds. However, what he notices on the trip south is "the incompleteness of all the signs, the satisfaction that their version said it all. I'd kept looking. . . for an equivalence that never came." The narrator's desire to find equivalencies extends beyond the radio: again and again he dreams that rather than being an outcast he is *like* the others, part of their community. All the signs, however, suggest that he is fated to be different: poverty forces him to be a Rocket Richard fan in a Boston Bruins' sweater (donated by the Schmitzes); he would like to believe that "I was a Deschênes, a Schmitz in the making," but he finds that the American Schmitzes "seemed blessed by a different branch of fate" which was not to be his. Most of all, he wants to believe in an equivalence between his father and Rocket Richard. The Rocket belongs to a tribe. People respect him. He's French Canadian and successful. Apparently he's a hero to the narrator's father as well, for tatooed upon his chest he sports "a front-faced Rocket, staring at an imaginary goalie and slapping a rising shot through a cloud of ice chips." The picture tells us that when the narrator dreams of the Rocket he is dreaming of his father as well. But Blaise narrators aren't allowed to hold their dreams too long. Someone or something must be there to shatter the fantasy and say: remember that you are "utterly alone" and that you are forever different. This time the reminder comes from the Schmitzes, who "pointed and laughed" at the tatoo, which they saw as "a kind of tribal marking." To the narrator, the tatoo (the father) becomes an embarrassment, and the fantasized equivalence between father and French-Canadian hero is ruthlessly destroyed. What he learns is that his father is the failed dreamer who had "put up the best, and the longest, show of his life" just to convince his brother-in-law that he was not an incurable drunk. Bad shows and thwarted dreams mark each story in Part I of *Tribal Justice*. "Broward Dowdy" — the amputated dream of lasting friendship; "Relief" — the drowned dream of creating an imaginative relief map that will endure; "Eddie Brewster" — the impossible dream of being French Canadian and fabulous; "Grids and Doglegs" — the clichéd dream of being a high school Bogart who will never own an American queen; "Rocket Richard" — the mutilated dream of the father who never made his goal.

The second section of *Tribal Justice* also concentrates on dreams.

Sometimes the vision is confused. "The Seizure" is an almost surreal-istic story told from shifting perspectives: at one point the narrator plays omniscient, at another his view is limited, at a third he sits back and lets dialogue speak for him, at a fourth we find a relatively straightforward, third-person account. Although Blaise demon-strates agility in each narrative form, he seems unable to decide how he wants these voices to cohere. So the story branches off in several directions. It begins by defining the personality of the seizer as it emerges in Malick. Because Malick is a type, rather than an indivi-dual, and because this story of seizure is in essence archetypal, the spatio-temporal boundaries remain purposefully undefined: "Where are we? North? East? Midwest? You cannot say." The next few pages introduce us to characters who are clearly meant to be the other types contributing to this Célinesque drama about death on the installment plan. There is Delman, who first appears as "a giant black man in a green uniform." There is Justin, the rich boss's son, who "lives for the school year to end, when he will decamp to France for his junior year." Later, there will be Mrs. Simmons (mistress to Malick), the deputy and, finally, the seized, the Szafransky's. After the second page, however, Blaise gets interested in these people as individuals, and as he begins to define their obsessions and delusions new stories begin to unfold which *are* rooted in time and place. The story about Margaret Malick getting calls from Mrs. Simmons about her lover. The story about Delman looking at *Life* magazine pictures of massacres and hovering his fantasies "between being a Cossack and being a revolutionary soldier." The story about Justin who wants to live in books, who can "picture himself in a left bank café reading, nervously puffing a rancid Gauloise."

Where are all these individual stories going? At first they seem to be organized around the day of the seizure: we will get to the Szafransky's and see them "like a giant tribe in undersized quarters" (Blaise is at home here). We will go right inside the house to repossess it, and we will see the filth, smell the stench, trip over "piles of toys, dishes, papers, and clothes" which litter the floor. We will pass by Szafransky quickly ("He smelled of unbrushed teeth"). But when we are inside, or while we are watching the broken furniture being carted out, the question comes back, nagging: why are all these people doing these things? To answer that question is to suggest what Blaise's original intent might have been. He seems to have begun with a story about oppression, and he seems to have wanted to say something about minorities — a concern which is present in much of his work. But Blaise could never leave his *types* alone, could never satisfy himself with defining them in terms of white and black, good and evil, oppressed and oppressor. As it turns out, everybody in the story is a bigot (Listen to the "bohunk" Szafranskys, who are ostensibly the oppressed, talk about "coon shooting" and Delman, the well-behaved "nigger," while Delman, in turn, looks at their hovel and thinks: *"Pump a few rounds into the kitchen")*. Universal complicity. Is *that* what Blaise was writing about? Or were the seizure's social implications left behind as Blaise began to see the story from yet another perspective: Justin Malick's? Justin is the kind of character that fascinates Blaise. He's a reader, a "thinker" who has the chance to apply his knowledge and make choices, a rich man's son who can act against the typology of oppression which surrounds him ("I don't make the rules," said the deputy. *"I do,"* thought Judd. *"God help me")*. Maybe he should help himself, but he doesn't, preferring to view the drama around him, like his own life, as a static picture in a gallery: "It's like a painting, you know?" Now most Blaise narrators retreat into art as an alternative to the rawness they know so well. But Judd never touches the rawness, and because he remains content to read about it he is ultimately condemned to his stupidity. "The whole world was winking behind his back." Ironically it is Justin's reading of Céline that colours the story's emphasis on prejudice and misanthropy, its attempt to seize upon "some definitive corruption." Judd fails to realize that the fiction which engrosses him is happening around him for real. Judd can't handle life. He can't handle Céline. At the end of the story he hasn't "seen something final" because he withdraws from the tragic implications of the tale. Or as he says: it's "As though everything that I can understand is radiating out from this little book, embracing more and more things that I can't understand, and I want to look away from all of it." Blaise has taken us far from the "gold watch band gleaming on a hairy wrist" that caught his eye at the start. When the seizure ends, we sense that he is beginning to isolate the question that he sidestepped all along: does intelligence demand moral responsibility, and, if so, how is that responsibility to be achieved?

Blaise is most concerned with a morality of *seeing*, with the perceptual choices the artist makes in his attempt to render his world with honesty. "Notes Beyond a History" is about one moral record of experience in which the narrator tries to find the "unacknowledged essence of things" which gives form to private and public time. He has written the *History of Hartley*. It's got all the facts. He can sit in his "air-conditioned" office "wrapped in tinted glass" and think about how Oshacola has been "humanized." But there is another kind of history, the narrator suggests, and "therein lies the rest of my story." The other history is creative and personal. It records the past in terms of memory and obsession and concentrates on the "mythic moment" which may define an entire period in one's life. The narrator's problem is that "Not only has the lake been civilized, but so has my memory, leaving only a memory of my memory as it was then." In his attempt to undo the civilized record of his roots, the narrator has to concentrate on "what I see with my eyes closed, books shut," has to perceive the imagined story beyond the recorded history: notes beyond a history.

The notes recreate the narrator's involvement with Theodora Rourke, a woman rumoured to have mixed blood and obscure, perhaps unsavoury, connections beyond Hartley in the daytime. To the narrator, Rourke is a magical, reclusive woman whose history is a secret. Big Mama, as she is called, may also be a symbolic figure who inhabits a place like an "auction house" filled with "paintings," "photos," "metal and porcelain objects that reflected the pale sunlight like the spires of a far-off, exotic city," and a "remarkable crucified Christ" gazing from the parlour wall. Soon the narrator is eating cake in an undeniable act of communion. Yet the parlour experience is by no means strictly Catholic in implication. Picture Rourke's house as a metaphor for imagination and the religious dimensions of the scene begin to harmonize with the historical contexts of the story. To enter Rourke's house is to be inside the mystery of memory, for in fact Rourke is surrounded by *things* whose "essence" is "unacknowledged" by the outside world. Everything in the house is mysterious, including the Christ on the wall. It is precisely the narrator's experience of this mystery which becomes the focal point of remembrance and a key releasing him from his all-too-explicable *History of Hartley*. Later in the story he tells us that, like Henry James, he is "a partisan of the broad sweep, of mystery that sweetens as its sources grow deep and dim." To go beyond the written history is to produce the "deep and dim" imaginative rendering of events associated with Rourke. To make *notes* is to pursue the story before the story, the mysterious entrance to the past which remains fiction, remains art. The narrator wants that fiction much more than his office, his job, and what he sees as a present "crumbling into foolishness." In celebrating Rourke's mysteriousness, he celebrates his own. The remembered journey down the river ("so deep into nature") in search of Rourke's secret is clearly a heart of darkness voyage that deliberately refuses light. "I live in the dark" Sutherland says, and we sense that he likes it that way. After all, without the mystery what story would he have told?

Gerald Gordon in "How I Became a Jew" also thrives on mystery, and he also relies on his imagination to release him from a troubling first day at school in Cincinnati. For "the spelling champ and fastest reader in Colquitt County, Georgia," Leonard Sachs Junior High is far from home. Rather than respect the fact that Gerald "is a borderline genius" as they did in Georgia, Mr. Terleski humiliates the transfer student who once helped his teacher assign grades. That's a bad blow to the Blaise narrator, who prides himself on his intelligence, and in this case, it's particularly bad because Gerald is singled out for ridicule, judo chops, and taunts as well. To his horror Gordon discovers that these jeering people are his classmates, that for the first time in his life he will be grouped with blacks and Jews, and that "for the first time in my life I knew that whatever answer I gave would be wrong." But Gordon can't stop being a Blaise narrator. He's a pest. He keeps asking questions and knows the answers to too many. He's polite (no matter how you beat him), slightly porky, and, like Normie in "Grids and Doglegs," he wears "gabardines." A total oddity in this place. But watch how familiar his response is to this acculturation crisis. He transforms the threatening day into the beginning of a utopian fantasy by concentrating on a name he hears in his second class: "*Israel, Israel, Israel*, and the dread of the days to come lifted, the days I would learn once and for all if Israel could really be real." The next day he'll be in the library, looking the country up. This day, however, Israel suggests a communal alternative to the isolation he feels in the new school, a commonalty described by Spiro when he speaks of Israeli children as "brothers and sisters" who "belong equally to every parent" and who inhabit a *kibbutz* where there is "No fighting, no namecalling, no sickness." It's a comforting dream, one that is even more inviting because of its fictional possibilities. As the principal says, there is "a long story" behind these Hebrews. And Gerald, who looks around at his Jewish classmates, feels "as though the Bible had come to life." Armed with the word, Gerald can begin to create an imagined world where he will be "straight and strong and tall" and safe.

53

"How I Became a Jew" is followed by "The March," a disappointing seventy-five-page novella strained by weak dialogue, a boring plot, and characters who become moral mouthpieces annoying in their drone. Blaise tries to fit in too much. A displaced French-Canadian narrator witnesses a series of personal and political confrontations which prompt him to affirm his heritage. In the process of "finding himself," Pierre Desjardins must reject his past, go to America, become an intellectual at Harvard, meet an American civil rights worker (his future wife), return to Quebec, fall in love with a burn-scarred Indian woman, identify with minorities, and arrive in Washington to join a protest march. Blaise's intent is obvious: this was to be a story about crossing cultural, linguistic, and racial frontiers which was structured as a pilgrimage seen by an overly sensitive "I" working against his sense that "nothing we had ever believed and no place that we had ever lived had truly been our choice." Ultimately, Pierre does choose, but by that point we don't care. What went wrong? Blaise writes most powerfully when he isolates a particular experience and allows the narrator to dwell on it, turn it, explore it, until poetic significance is distilled from what might normally appear to be mundane. In "The March," the focus is too broad for the poetry to be effective: we keep waiting for a concentrated rendering of awareness which seldom comes.

The third section of *Tribal Justice* comes back to surer footings which show Blaise's skill at isolating the ironies inherent in daily life. Set in and around Montreal, the three stories also provide an appropriate locale for Blaise to examine the bicultural tensions that contribute to his narrator's social stance. But it is more than a troubled social perspective which makes these stories work. They are drawn together by visions of futility and failure, by voices which keep asking: why is everything I dream about inevitably destroyed?

The question certainly obsesses the narrator of "At the Lake," an academic who, lured by "the dream of a northern retreat" is hooked into buying a waterfront cottage in the Laurentians—"the essence of all I wanted from a place in the woods." What he has really purchased is the *fiction* of having a cottage on a remote lake, and, like many of Blaise's narrators, he tries to make the fiction his retreat, seeing his northern weekends as an escape into the symbolism of the frontier where he can act out his dream of "manly things" ("I wanted the lake accessible yet remote, I wanted my cabin rustic but livable"). Inevitably, the experience of the experience of owning a cottage takes prominence. And the narrator, ever ready to see himself as a cliché, reminds us often that he knows he knows about the dream of North: "I'd always wanted to believe that somewhere not too far from where I would settle, *quincailliers* read the classics and fished (and academics worked with their hands and fell asleep sore and exhausted)." It doesn't take him long to realize that the dream won't work and that, unlike Serge, he will always be an outsider, that in fact he is not "more aware a thousand times of ravages, impurity, and decay." The "battle" to civilize the forest, he soon discovers, is "overwhelming" because what he is really battling is himself: "I had come to see myself mirrored in my property; each summer I would try frantically to keep pace with nature" and each summer he would lose a little more ground, until the dream shatters, as it always does in Blaise's fiction. The narrator dives into the lake, looking for redemption, but he surfaces with leeches hanging from his waist "like a cartridge belt." Being at the lake leaves him "shaking with rage and disillusionment."

"He Raises Me Up" is a mutability story centring on another disillusioned narrator who claims the "satisfaction" of "recognizing the comedy" of being stranded with his wife in a broken-down new car "on a deserted cloverleaf in the dead of winter." The opening claim is obviously ironic, a last-ditch attempt to deny the personal defeat implicit in the barren, frigid landscape. Here is a man who measures his life, not by coffee spoons, but by the cars he has owned, and what he discovers on this night is that the latest model has suffered a seizure, "a stroke, a heart attack, in the prime of life, the blowing of a cerebral gasket." "Cars are an apt measurement of the inner man," he says, so we look to the vehicle to find the man and discover his private dream: to maintain his "Posture in the universe" like Prufrock, to be fit like "An oiled, greased, rustless, spotless, vacuumed, silent car." And then the reality which he can't ignore: "'Your motor's jammed'" and he is jammed, a pathetic "*Clown*" confronted at every turn by his own absurd values, by the naïve "simplicity of my dream of merely getting home in a well-groomed car."

Where is home? In a story which turns a "Finished" car into a metaphor of human death, home is most appropriately associated with the grave. The story closes with an image of the "broken" car as hearse in tow, housing the narrator "stretched out on the front seat" beside his wife, thinking "how peaceful is this surrender." His surrender comes as no surprise, for he is filled with thoughts about decay and mortality. "Teeth," he tells us, are, like his car, "Inescapable indices of the inner man." But the teeth here are rotten: "my mouth was botched and those pulpy bitches were all but doomed." "The dentist, like a priest," puts it more bluntly: " 'You were dying, you know.' " He didn't know, but the "inner damage" he discovers on the freeway affects him metaphysically, makes him conscious of "the frailty of identity" and allows him to articulate what is certainly the crucial point: "Perhaps when your time has come, all the care is superficial."

"Among the Dead," the last story in *Tribal Justice*, prepares us for the narrator's sudden recognition that "I'm in danger." Within the urban context of the story, and surrounded by "city walls," man becomes an endangered species living in a prison of failed dreams. "The Dead" of the title are not only the St. Vincent de Paul inmates whom the narrator visits "Because I am a journalist and I want to reach people directly." The "perpetual solitary confinement" associated with the prison also becomes a metaphor for an entire society deluded into believing that it is free. When the narrator says that "We are each other's hostages," he is referring to every member of this "new society" which thrives on "nuance and taboo, madness, and waste." The equation between the men inside and those outside is made more concrete by the opening emphasis on *bongoûtisme*. Outside the walls, we learn, "Our dream had always been salvation and *bonheur*." Inside the walls, the dream persists, but in forms slightly more "transcendent": "a new planet, a new liberated man." In both cases, however, the dream fails. "Most of us," the narrator says, "live with broken hearts," and later he confesses that "most of us" includes him: "my heart is broken like everyone else's."

What happened to make this man who was raised on *bongoûtisme* "dream my immolation"? To answer this question is to approach the death which most concerns this troubled speaker—the death of style. The story begins by defining *bongoûtisme* as a failed *life*-style full of boredom and "unrelenting" sameness. *Bongoûtisme* is "the worst of both worlds: the suspicions and ignorance of the *petit commercant*, with the arrogant sprawl of America." This is the style the narrator was raised in, the style he wants to escape. So he dreams that "Because I work on a liberal paper" he has gone beyond *bongoûtisme*, that he is capable of being "an easy ironist" with a "sensitive eye" to beauty. But this man has the Blaise syndrome. Who can believe his claims? Chances are that like other Blaise narrators, this man's postures say more about what he has failed to become than what he is. In fact, his life is governed by the preoccupation with style that emerges in the final words he speaks. If he is "Among the Dead," it is because he is imprisoned by his need to see himself as a character in any story but his own. He will be a martyr preaching to prison heathens ("I see myself as a Jesuit instructing the Iroquois"). He will be the man who can adopt the prisoners' personae and say "I know these girls" who have come to set us free. I can see myself. I know myself. I am different and, therefore, kin to these men who shun *bongoûtisme* and "pride themselves on their realism, their shrewdness, their nihilism." I am part of the outcast elite: "Half the time, even if the guard above us were listening, he wouldn't understand a word." Is he really confronting himself, or has he become the embodiment of the *bongoûtisme* which is "a kind of rampant self-expressionism that quickly becomes a caricature"? And is his identification with the inmates not prompted by his desire to withdraw from the very society he says he wants to change? There is always a moment of truth, an instant in which the Blaise narrator stands back and sees the dream's illness. In "Among the Dead" the narrator finds the truth outside the haven of St. Vincent de Paul. "It torments me," he admits, "that I failed to see." As *Tribal Justice* closes, we watch him driving into the "maze of constricted ruts" that has always marked his life.

How will the drive end? You can look back over Clark Blaise's short fiction and read your way out of the maze. You can say, here are the dichotomies which form the mural's gut. And you can begin chopping at the stories until you get beneath the mask to see the livid, pensive face. But when you get that far the fiction turns and walks away, mocks the stupid assumption that its ambivalent *ethos* will yield a single truth, a single stance that can be called Clark Blaise. He's there, but he ghosts by in abstraction, shadings, philosophical nuance. You track him in his darkness, trying to find the lair, and you find it, but it's empty. So you walk down the trail and begin to wonder: how does a Clark Blaise story *really* feel?

NOTES

[1]   My textual references throughout this reading are to Clark Blaise, *A*

North American Education (Toronto: Doubleday, 1973), and *Tribal Justice* (Toronto: Doubleday, 1974).

2   Frank Davey, "Clark Blaise," in *From There to Here: A Guide to English-Canadian Literature Since 1960. Our Nature-Our Voices* II (Erin, Ont.: Porcépic, 1974), p. 55.

3   William H. New, "Fiction," in *Literary History of Canada: Canadian Literature in English*, gen. ed. and introd. Carl F. Klinck (Toronto: Univ. of Toronto Press, 1976), III, p. 259.

4   Michael E. Darling, "Of Time and Memory," *Essays on Canadian Writing*, No. 2 (Spring 1975), p. 54.

5   Clark Blaise, "To Begin, To Begin," in *The Narrative Voice: Short Stories and Reflections by Canadian Authors*, ed. John Metcalf (Toronto: McGraw-Hill Ryerson), 1972, p. 22.

John Metcalf

Unburdening the mystery

ANYONE WHO IS INTERESTED in reading criticism of John Metcalf's short fiction will discover a curious fact: aside from some excellent commentary by Barry Cameron,[1] no serious discussions of Metcalf's art have appeared. Why is this so? One answer lies in the fact that Metcalf refuses to be ornate—his prose is so chaste, so uncompromisingly direct that exegesis often seems to be redundant. Yet to accept Metcalf's stories at face value is to ignore the extraordinary narrative compression which multiplies the weight of every word and to miss the *ideas* Metcalf develops from his concentration on *things*. Another reason Metcalf's stories have been overlooked is that they are, by contemporary standards, relatively traditional in form: there is no trendiness here, no straining to impose deconstructions, no hide-and-seek metaphors, doors to labyrinths, or visionary bric-a-brac. Metcalf isn't fancy. He believes that a plot should be interesting, mysterious, and built with dovetailed quality that will endure. He is concerned with the morality of his characters and their culture. He likes to set his stories realistically by concentrating on the details which define time and place. Most important, he is preoccupied with a well-worn theme: the relationship between art and human experience. For Metcalf this relationship is elusive, problematic, and in need of constant redefinition. Consequently his stories return again and again to explore the nature of aesthetic process, and to find the ingredients from which his own art is composed. These ingredients can be discerned by examining the three kinds of stories Metcalf tends to write.

Metcalf articulates the basic components of his art in stories about young boys or adolescents who, in moments of troubling recognition, confront the mysteries of time, mortality, and sex. I think here of "Early Morning Rabbits," "The Tide Line," and "Keys and

Watercress." Because the enigmas posed by nature are recognized but not resolved, these stories are appropriately presented through a moderated third-person viewpoint which reflects the central character's naïve perceptions and thoughts. This technique allows Metcalf to texture and impregnate his settings without intruding upon the frame to offer guidance or interpretation. Yet pattern abounds. Through word repetition, emphases on colour shifts, and juxtaposition of phenomena, Metcalf illuminates his young male heroes' awakening. The child, as we are told in "The Teeth of My Father," is involved *"In nothing more or less that the act of defining his identity."* [2] But Metcalf's initiation stories — rooted in the interplay of nature, time, and sex — also define the ingredients of the mature writer's craft.

As Metcalf's characters get older they become conscious of the aesthetic implications of their daily acts, and, finally, they turn into artists pre-occupied with the aesthetic justification of *all* their acts. In the second group of stories I will discuss ("Beryl," "The Lady Who Sold Furniture," "Girl in Gingham," and "Gentle As Flowers Make the Stones"), Metcalf concentrates on the experiences of men who are better equipped to interpret the puzzling events which befall them. The central characters in these stories have achieved a certain educational or professional status. They are university students, or teachers, or antique appraisers, or published poets. What was once a naïve fascination with decay and destruction has become a pointed concern with mortality and its metaphors. Time is no longer contained in the startling incident of a day but has broadened to include the web of memory as it gives form to human encounter. Things have now been graced with moral significance and the protagonist tries to confer identity upon the world by naming its objects and inhabitants. These changes suggest a broadening of awareness beneficial to the developing artist's voice. But the characters in these stories aren't happy. For one reason or another they refuse to act on the knowledge they have gained. Metcalf won't grant them first-person consciousness because they are not yet responsible enough to speak for themselves. In these stories the third-person narrator is distanced and somewhat critical of the characters and their world. He is concerned with the debased relationship between art and society, with the perversion of taste, with the inevitable loss of childlike perception that was unhampered by knowledge of change. His voice therefore tends toward the elegiac and satiric; elegiac because lost youth is mourned, satiric because contemporary culture is attacked for utterly corrupting the value placed on art. What must Metcalf's young men do to earn their own narrative voice?

This question can be answered by examining a third set of stories: "The Years in Exile," "The Teeth of My Father," and "Private Parts: A Memoir." In this group the central characters are writers whose first-person narratives explicitly and implicitly comment on the discovery of self through art. The basic forms of reference have not changed. Metcalf continues to stress the interdependence of ideas and things, the transformation in consciousness brought on by time, and the impact of culture upon craftsmanship. But in the hands of these self-conscious speakers these concerns are heightened, savoured, expanded toward their metaphorical potential until the telling of the story begins to resemble a theory of story-telling. Through the confessional structure of their tales, Metcalf's narrators now insist that private recollection provides the best means of approaching an uncertain present. Consequently, the time scheme of these stories encompasses decades rather than days, just as the spatial boundaries include several "auto-biographical" landscapes perceived from the vantage point of now.

It is not only the superimposition of tenses and places which broadens the narrators' scope but also their tendency to withdraw from their tale to comment on the success or failure of their telling. This critical impulse is by no means restricted to personal form: Metcalf's artists judge the work of other artists and comment forcefully on historical and geographical shifts in taste. And the closer they get to the present (the nearer they get to North America), the less they like what they see: people praying to their televisions, people ignorant of tradition, *kitsch* masquerading (and being applauded) as genuine art. By this point we suspect what their response to this contemporary Fall will be. The past will assume new resonance as cultivated, creative ground; the present will show us a wasteland full of loneliness, knowledge, and pain. These contrasts may suggest that Metcalf's most involved first-person stories verge toward allegory, a movement perfectly in keeping with the narrators' desire to reach the imaginative centre of their work by translating images through remembrance. When memory is absent, or unrelated to art, the landscape wears an entirely different face. To illustrate this difference I want to return to the first group of stories I have identified and concentrate on how they reveal the basis of Metcalf's aesthetic.

"Early Morning Rabbits" is an initiation story which centres on its young protagonist's first real confrontation with death. The title directs us to see his awakening within the context of the natural world. David is a city boy visiting Auntie Mary and Uncle Joe in the country. The rural setting is crucial because it signifies a change in David's habits and perspective. The link between foreign place and altered understanding is firmly established in the opening two paragraphs through a moderated third-person voice which reflects David's thoughts and sensations upon rising in a bed away from home:

> David was suddenly awake and staring at a patch of sunlight on the wallpaper. For a second, he missed his chest of drawers and the green pottery elephant that stood on the white runner. And then he took a deep breath. Arching his back as high as it would go, he dropped and floundered in the feather bed.
> He turned over and snuffed the smell of the heavy linen sheets. It was different from home. Houses had different smells. Auntie Mary smelled different from his mother.

Notice how the act of being "suddenly awake" is immediately connected with David's "staring" at "a patch of sunlight." The first sentence anticipates the rude awakening experienced by David when he later witnesses the "seeping eye" of the wounded rabbit, and frames the narrative in terms of gradually illuminated perception. I say "gradually" because it is only toward the end of the story that David's eyes are truly opened. In the beginning his knowledge of the room, of its foreignness, arises through his sense of smell (consider the placement, in the second paragraph, of the words "smell," "smells," and "smelled" in their relation to the word "different" which is repeated three times). The emphasis on "different" suggests that for David this will be an extraordinary day; in fact, the opening scene, though apparently couched in innocent images, contains a real sense of foreboding: like a trapped or wounded animal, David "dropped and floundered" *in* the bed.

Within eight lines Metcalf has established the structure he will develop. The story will link the shift from sleep to wakefulness with a growing awareness of death and the passage of time. David has risen early to fulfill a dream: he will prove himself to Uncle Joe by "hunting all day." He will be the big game hunter tracking more than pottery elephants. But as Joe points out, "city boys don't know everything," and David is certainly confused about killing. In the feed shed, for example, there was "a long knife with a strange fat blade and a black handle that was used for killing pigs." David plays with it, but puts it back "because he felt wrong." He'd also caught an eel, but "he hadn't told his uncle. It was just that somehow he hadn't wanted to mention it." On this morning, however, he is determined to be A Man, to satisfy Uncle Joe when he says " 'Let's feel your muscles, then, to see if you'll be a farmer.' " David probably won't be a farmer. But he does manage to shoot a rabbit and the kill moves him one step further away from childhood. In anticipation of this move, the day is punctuated by temporal signs aligned with death. There is "the ticking of the black clock on the mantelpiece" (which David hears after thinking about pig slaughter), and later, the same black clock is seen showing "five minutes to seven" (David notices it after remembering how he killed an eel). Even the landscape speaks of death. When David looks back from "the top field" he sees that "the trees and bushes were all mysteriously still," and later, as he comes closer to the rabbit, "the stones showed white and fawn, broken recently." The broken stones' colouring, of course, antici-pates the broken rabbit's "fawn-white belly." Metcalf is implying that David's discovery of the rabbit colours his understanding of the world, or, as the narrator puts it: "The seeping eye" of the wounded animal "seemed to grow, . . . growing in its wounded brownness till it filled the world." The "seeping eye" is obviously symbolic of a transformation in David's own perception. And the rabbit's squeal-ing, which sounded like "chalk on board" (in school?), is clearly meant to associate the object of the hunt with David's new know-ledge about the interdependence of life and death. The rabbit, we note, is half dead and half alive: "Its front paws were folded under it, but its back legs ran and tore at the earth in a frenzy of escape." The last sentence perfectly sums up the bifocal vision which David has obtained. He stands there watching the "running, running legs of the still body."

David's transformation is not only apparent in this final act of watching; it is traced throughout the story as Metcalf records the boy's changing reactions to farm life. At first, the place is filled with pleasant rural sounds and comforting alliteration. David hears "hens gargling in the yard," "Clogs clacked across the cobble-stones," "pails clanking and the door of the feedshed screeching open on its rusty runners." The hens are even presented as enter-tainers. They "clustered in falling pyramids like the acrobats at the Hippodrome." Near these sights and sounds David is safe. But the further he gets from the house, the more threatening things become ("Each clump of weeds, each thistle and frond of bracken became a bobbing pigeon or a crouched rabbit. At each alarm he froze, his lungs straining, the thud of his heart in his throat"). When David finds the rabbit, he no longer thinks of the farm, and the images of his city home have long been left behind. A common pattern in Metcalf's fiction is beginning to emerge: a young boy is lured away from the things or people he knows to a place he has never been. There, he sees something that troubles him deeply, something that allows him to realize that green pottery elephants on white runners don't last forever.

Like "Early Morning Rabbits," "The Tide Line" captures one boy's encounter with death when he finds a decayed seagull on a Bournemouth beach. And like David, Charles makes his discovery alone, away from his parents who have isolated themselves from the crowded promenade. "His mother had said that she hadn't the slightest intention of sharing her holiday with *other people*." Her attitude towards those people indicates the kind of family in which Charles has been raised. They consider themselves to be refined. They want to keep away from the "*disgusting* lizards" on the beach and removed from the disgusting tourists on the promenade with their "inflated ducks and plastic sea monsters." They choose hotels with "trees in brass tubs." They want to be *in* nature without touching it. Note Father's objective description of the lizard which fascinates Charles: " 'They're not rare,' he said, 'but they're extremely local in their distribtuion.' " And listen to Mother protect-ing Charles from the elements: " 'Can I take my hat off?' said Charles." " 'No, dear.' " " 'Can I take my shirt off now?' " " 'When it gets warmer.' " " 'Can I play on the rocks?' " " 'No. It's too dan-gerous. And you'll get grubby.' " Charles isn't encouraged to enjoy himself, but he *has* been encouraged to *write*. His father (pre-occupied with newspaper and "silver propelling pencil") has given Charles a pen "for coming top of his class," and with this pen, Charles thinks, he will copy Father's words "in his holiday book." Given the emphasis placed on mind rather than matter, it is not surprising to find Charles transforming experience according to what he has gleaned from books. Alone in his bed, he imagines the lizard, "reared up on its front legs like one of the white stone lions in his father's picture book of Greece."

By devoting the opening pages to these images of security, withdrawal, and literacy, Metcalf establishes a basis of contrast for Charles' contact with the physical world he discovers away from the umbrellas and "beach bag heavy with bottles of suntan oil." "Against his mother's instructions," he "filled his pockets, cramming them with jade-green ovals of sea-smoothed glass." The tide line seems magical; certainly, Charles is "fascinated by its strange treasures." But we sense that these treasures also say something about time. Charles is surrounded by evidence of birth and death and transience: "clusters of whelk eggs" and "mermaids' purses" lie beside "shrivelled seaweed," "refuse and sea shells." David strokes "driftwood branches" which "implored the air like drowning arms and fingers." The juxtaposed images prepare us for the climactic appearance of the seagull which, like David's prey in "Early Morning Rabbits," seems to be both dead and alive: "One wing was spread, perfect, as if in flight. The rest of the body was crumpled, stained black and yellow with oil." On one hand the stained bird's appearance comments on the disfiguring impact of society upon nature, a form of defilement which began long ago when Hengistbury Head, "a brooding, massive headland," was first "carved with the dikes and barrows of the early people." On the other hand, the seagull serves to awaken Charles' perception of his immediate surroundings. He is no longer imagining absent things but apprehending phenomena through all his senses. Consider the way in which the paragraph that follows Charles' discovery stresses seeing, smelling, hearing, and touching:

> Charles crouched staring at the fragile bones and yellowed feathers. The sun, climbing towards noon, beat down into the wedge formed by the black rocks and cliffwall. The air was rank with the smell of the rotting barnacles. The wash of the sea was muted and distant and in the still heat he could imagine the sounds of the spurting sand fleas. The pebbles cut into his knees. He reached out to touch the bird.

The words make it clear that Charles' world has changed; he senses that the tide line is somehow in him. So when he suddenly sees a living seabird, he finds that its "raucous cry" is "clamouring in his head."

Does the clamour change him? Remember that in "Early Morning Rabbits" the shattered eye seemed to alter David's whole world. But any change in his behaviour is left for us to imagine. Similarly, we know that the dead seagull will colour Charles' future, but now he retreats, huddling "into the shadow until he could feel the rock cutting into his back" and "flinging" the treasures in his pocket "down onto the sand and pebbles near the dead bird." In search of safety, he looks for "the shape of his father and the red of his mother's bathing suit." Yet the important point is this: "he did not join his parents"; instead, "he watched the orderly progression of the waves" and "clutched his fountain pen." With his other hand "he patted the sand, drawing designs with his fingers and then smoothing them out." Charles is not yet ready to consider the implications of what he has seen, but half of him connects with the sand which becomes a new kind of "holiday book" holding man's transient designs.

"Keys and Watercress" is the last, and strangest piece in this first group of stories. Once again, we are back to a character named David, and we find him fishing for eels when an eccentric old man appears. The man invites David to tea "In the house across the bridge — in the house with the big garden." David is uncertain (" 'My mother'll be angry if I'm late' ") but he agrees to follow this man who has been talking about the proper names of things, writing with his fountain pen, and displaying his large flat watch, which he calls a Hunter. The house is as odd as its owner. Books are piled helter-skelter, the biggest mirror David had ever seen "stood above the fireplace," and a stuffed lion is displayed in the "long," "dark," "stuffy" room which, David thinks, "smelled like his grandma."

Soon the ritual of tea takes a curious turn: it begins to resemble a lesson in which the old man talks about matters of "taste," "texture," and "vision" while he writes out "facts" for David in the notebook he repeatedly pulls from his pocket. Then the old man closes the red curtains and takes out "three small leather sacks" containing "hundreds of keys; long rusted keys, flat keys, keys with little round numbers tied to them, keys bunched together on rings, here and there sparkling new Yale keys, keys to fit clocks and keys for clockwork toys." The keys are obviously connected with time, and the "red rust" which clings to them emphasizes that David is surrounded by signs of duration. When the old man displays the bullet cut from his leg in the Boer War, we know that he is inextricably linked with historical time as well. But when he shows David his leg wound, where "The flesh sank deep, seamed and puckered, shiny, livid white and purple, towards a central pit," we sense that the story is about more than a quirky man who wants to have tea with a young boy. The objects in the story are imbued with vague Freudian symbolism: the appearance of the scar, the darkened room, the keys, the references to eel-fishing, and most peculiar of all, the "blood" which "welled into the pit" as David rips a scab, "enjoying the tingling sensation as it tore free." Whether the opening scene anticipates defloration is unclear, but there is no doubt that the imagery which introduces the story, and David, is united with the imagery devoted to the old man at the end. His scar, like David's, has a "central pit" that is eventually probed.

A sexual awakening? Perhaps. But David's experiences seem to be more involved with aesthetic awareness. From this point of view the old man may be seen as a teacher whose keys symbolize entrance into the world of genuine art. As he tells David: "'I've tried to teach you. I've tried to teach you.'" During the day, he sets down several points that the artist might bear in mind:

1. Know the *"proper name"* of things.
2. When you know the name, "write it down."
3. Pay attention to watches. Know the meaning of *time*.
4. "Always be attentive."
5. "Always accumulate *facts*." "Facts, eh? *Facts*."
6. Surround yourself with books.
7. Realize that "it's not simply a matter of taste."
8. Know "about texture."
9. Know "about vision."
10. Look carefully "in the mysterious depths of the mirror."
11. "Pay attention!"
12. Know the meaning of history.

Not surprisingly, these twelve points describe the major ingredients of Metcalf's art. And if we reconsider "Early Morning Rabbits" and "The Tide Line" in terms of these keys, we can see that

Metcalf has been using them to open up his stories all along. But because his characters are young, and afraid, they hold the keys reluctantly, hesitating before the door. The resolution of "Early Morning Rabbits" only *implies* that David will cross thresholds. Charles in "The Tide Line" makes a partial move by refusing to join his parents at the story's close. And David in "Keys and Watercress" actually makes it *through* the door, though "At first, in his panic, he wrenched the doorknob the wrong way."

II

By way of introducing the second kind of story Metcalf writes I want to consider the aesthetic implications of "Beryl," a transition piece that marks its central character's thwarted sense of the relations between sex, society, and art. Although there is no evidence to establish the fact that "David" in this story is an older version of the boy in "Early Morning Rabbits" and "Keys and Watercress," it seems reasonable to assume that Metcalf is following a single character in various stages of development. David explains to Beryl that "he was about to begin his second year at university and that one had to go there for three years; that most of his time was spent in reading books, discussing them with his teachers, and then in writing essays about them." He is "working away his summer vacation at the Leicester Co-Operative Bakery." The situation allows Metcalf to contrast David's middle-class, suburban consciousness with the working-class concerns of the bakery's permanent employees who have little time for "earnest discussions of the politics or sanity of Ezra Pound and the moral force of F. R. Leavis' criticism."

The contrast takes several forms. David lives in an area with "street lights" and "blank suburban houses with their lawns and rockeries behind trim privet hedges," but the "industrial park" which he reaches by bus (full of "people still half asleep in the fug of body heat and cigarette smoke") shows him another side of life that is not trim and proper but inescapably crude. Mr. Benson, David's supervisor, collects Nazi insignia and sports "the tatoo of a spread-eagled lady" under his "greasy wool vest." And the bakery workers amuse themselves with vulgar repartee full of sexual innuendo:

When Greg, the electrician, came through, he'd yell to

the machinists,

"Any of you girls need an adjustment?"

And they would shriek with laughter.

"Hark at 'im."

"It'd take a bigger man than you."

As the exchange suggests, the difference between David and these factory workers involves language as well as sensibility. David talks to Beryl "about Chinese art and poetry" and speaks to himself in words borrowed from Cervantes and Keats. Raised on "Romantic books and films," David is an oddity in the workers' eyes. Worst of all, he seems to be devoted to a curious work ethic which condemns inefficiency. Or as Mr. Benson says after he has watched David filling the bakery trays:

"All very well for you, boy. You'll be gone in a few weeks. And the time for this job'll have gone down by two hours. We has to stay on after you're back with your books and very nicely thank you with a bit of pocket money. You take your rhythm from me, boy."

The point, of course, is that David never will be able to find Benson's rhythm, and, seduced by romantic visions of Beryl as the woman of his dreams ("he imagined bathing her. Champagne glasses. Soaping her shoulders, the nape of her neck") he is inevitably led to follow a non-existent ideal. The reference to Don Quixote ("Faint heart never won fair lady") is revealing and by no means coincidental. Clad in the shining armour of his "loud boots," David thinks he can transcend "that far away world, that Beryl-less world of seminars and tutorials." But the fact is that David thrives on thought; and his failure lies in the belief that satisfaction can be found only through literature and art. So to impress Beryl ("She'd been really interested in art," she said, but "work was more interesting, wasn't it, and you earned good money") he offers her "a reproduction of a Chinese scroll painting." It showed "Two ducks on a river bank, three or four dark strokes of reeds, in the background the suggestion of a mountain." David never realizes that his gift, like his Quixotic behaviour, is only an imitation of the real thing. But Beryl likes the painting ("'go nice over the dressing table it will'") and seems to be entirely won over (meanwhile David is rehearsing the ultimate seduction scene, "rehearsals ranging from the perverse to the pastoral"). The connection between sex and art (rendered here as artifice) cannot be missed. In his first-person stories about true artists Metcalf will establish a genuine relationship between sexual experience and aesthetic achievement. In "Beryl," however, David's concept of the art/life tension is still naïve, and consequently, his real aesthetic prowess is limited. He has a sense of the past, but he conceives of private history as a force to be ignored ("he turned facedown the wedding photo of his father and mother"); he has some knowledge of the religious implications of his sexual training, but he would prefer not to think of the "kisses and fumbling at the rear of the Methodist Church following ping-pong at the Youth Club." He wants to live out his dream, never realizing that Beryl is not elegant but ignorant, coarse, and lewd. She, in turn, wants to believe that David cares for her, when in fact he is pursuing the enticing woman in a poem.

Obviously the relationship is headed for failure. David follows Beryl "towards that part of the city where the streets were still cobbled and the hosiery mills and shoe factories stood black and massive against the sky," and we begin to anticipate a resolution that will be as unromantic as the industrial landscape. David is reluctant to admit it, but "gran's" house and its surroundings completely shatter the illusions. After all, the place stands in gloom, "Washing-lines criss-crossed the yard," and "In the cobbled centre stood a row of outhouses" which David "did not like." As it turns out, Beryl has been right about one thing all along. David *is* "soft," and finally he admits that sex with Beryl won't work. " 'I can't,' " he says, " 'I've recently had an operation.' " The reason David "can't" is that everything in Gran's place reminds him of reality. Reality is not "The Eve of St. Agnes" but the "Three Anglican vicars" who were "discussing modern attitudes to miracles" on television. Reality is not *Don Quixote* but "a chase sequence" on "the commercial channel." The imposition of crudity on romance is suggested most concretely when David looks at Beryl's "spread hair" (the hair he has adored as the essence of her beauty) while "On the screen" a thug's legs are spread: "a braced and straddled man was being frisked by a police officer." And does the "spread" of Beryl's hair bear any relation to the picture of the "spreadeagled" lady on Mr. Benson's tatooed chest? Metcalf is too finicky a writer to miss the connection. In the end, he consciously corrupts all the pictures with which Beryl and

David are associated, and therefore suggests that their final inability to communicate arises from their handicapped relation to both art and life. In Beryl's words: " 'All I wish is that you hadn't given me those ducks.' "

Presumably David will reach a clearer understanding of his impulses when he graduates and is forced to deal with the 'real world' on a full-time basis. Certainly, the correspondence between leaving school and entering into concrete experience is central to "The Lady Who Sold Furniture," a novella whose central character, Peter Hendricks, has completed his university training and accepted a teaching post at the Gartree Comprehensive School. The story is told from a third-person perspective which has privileged access to Peter's thoughts about his present situation, his life as a student, and his continuing relationship with Jeanne, a crafty woman whom he has known for years as both friend and lover. At first glance "The Lady Who Sold Furniture" appears to be a mild, amusing tale which traces Peter's gradual recognition of the fact that Jeanne is a con artist who survives by selling off the furniture in the houses she has been hired to manage. But the closer we read, the more we realize that Metcalf is concerned with the nature of identity as it develops in relation to art, society, and remembrance. In this respect, the aliases which Jeanne adopts—the transience of her identity—imply the central problem with which Peter is faced: he must discover who he is.

No Metcalf character makes this discovery without becoming sensitive to time's passage and attentive to the value of craftsmanship. Peter's personal growth is set within a broad temporal frame. The action does not encompass a day (as it did in "Early Morning Rabbits," "The Tide Line," and "Keys and Watercress"), or several days (as it did in "Beryl") but many weeks in the physical course of events and several years through the process of memory. This extended temporal setting is united with a shifting sense of place as Peter moves from Jeanne's house, to the school building, to Jeanne's father's "cottage near the sea" to the "Compton-Smythe residence," all the while remembering other landscapes, other states of mind. The conjunction between time, space, and art becomes apparent when we realize that through Jeanne's criminal activities Peter learns to judge the quality of genuine antiques, "the class of piece," as Mr. Arkle puts it. It comes as no surprise to find Mr. Arkle making another point: high quality art *endures*. Arkle is not formally edu-

71

cated (note his tendency to mispronounce words) but he does know that the mahogany table in Jim's house is " 'a different class of piece altogether.' " He invites Peter to feel "under the table" and to note that he is touching " 'A bit of real craftsmanship' " because the piece has " 'None of your glue. None of your nails. None of your screws,' " but " '*Joints and pegs.*' " " 'Manogony,' " he says, " 'goes on for ever.' " Arkle is not only talking about how to appreciate craftsmanship; his words perfectly isolate the temporal dilemma confronting Peter: he is surrounded by evidence of change which forces him to realize that unlike "manogony," he will not go on "forever," and he tries different ways to stop time and stave off age. At this point in his life, he is trying particularly hard because his new job makes him all too conscious of the youth and freedom associated with his student years. Jim states the problem most succinctly:

> "So, you've left the Alma Mater?" said Jim, helping himself to the ham. "The halcyon days are over. Out into the cold, harsh world. Nose to the grindstone, eh?"

Jim misquotes the Prince's lines from *Henry IV*, but he tries to say that "If all the year were playing holidays, / To sport would be as tedious as to work." The argument treads on Peter's patience; he *would* like to play on and on.

At first, we watch him noticing time, trying to ignore it, or doing his best to make it stand still. For example, Peter sees the change in Jeanne's appearance. She looks older "Without make-up and in the morning light, her face was pale and gaunt" and "The lines seemed deeper drawn than he'd remembered." To deny the lines, he retreats into remembrance and the narrative backtracks to "that afternoon of another summer when Jeanne had suddenly come into their room with an enamel bowl of ice and four bottles of *Chablis.*" The other summers will survive as long as Peter stays away from school, away from the institution which will destroy the halcyon days. But consider what happens when he decides to "time the route" to school. The bus trip over, he passes "a small public garden which was surrounded by a wire-mesh fence." And what he sees inside suggests that he cannot escape the vision of age, youth, and time: "An old man," "Five boys on bicycles," and a "floral clock." Later, Peter and Jeanne help Anna build a dam to block a stream (stopped water, Metcalf knows, inevitably means stopped life). For a moment, in this country setting removed from Gartree Comprehensive and Jim's house (the walls of which are marred by evidence of bygone friends, bygone years) time does stop. Peter (consciously?) forgets to remove his wristwatch and it fills with water from the "muddied stream." "He undid the soggy strap and held the watch to his ear. It had stopped." The dam was holding. But no sooner does the trio walk away than the dam breaks: "The rising water was overflowing, seeping and trickling forward beneath the roots, glinting in the twilight." Contrast this scene with Peter's first day at school. Miss Brice makes it clear that the job calls for absolute punctuality:

> "Both of these are due in no later than ten-thirty this morn-
> ing."
> "Ten-thirty," said Peter.
> "On the dot," said Miss Brice.

During the day, Peter meets his colleagues, all of whom seem to be, like the secretary, pre-occupied with time. While Tony Rogers "glanced at his watch" two other teachers engage in a complicated discussion about a new travel route to school which, one says, will "often save you two or three minutes." By the end of the day, Peter is anxiously watching the clock and thinking, "thirteen minutes to go before the end of the lesson."

The placement of the school scene is crucial to an understanding of Peter's development. The Gartree Comprehensive experience lies at the story's centre. Before his classroom initiation, Peter can ignore the clock. We watch him hiding in his past as he "remembered... suddenly, vividly, a story in a comic" he had savoured as a child. After he has been through the lesson, however, he hears ticking wherever he goes. Even at the Compton-Smythe place, far away from school, he stands "listening to the tick of the grandfather clock." And "Somewhere in the bedroom a clock was ticking," while "Peter lay listening to the tick."

What is it that so profoundly alters Peter's involvement with time? Recall that after receiving instructions from Miss Brice, Peter stood in the staff room and looked at the letter rack. Significantly, "His name was not there." The detail suggests that Peter has not yet found his place, his name, his identity. In order to do so he must develop not only a willingness to recognize change, but also the ability to make moral choices. Although Peter initially senses that Jeanne's covert activities are wrong (note that she does not have a single name, and presumably never will have one) he makes no objection to her fraud. But after the day at Gartree his stance alters. He doesn't openly condemn Jeanne, but his thoughts and actions make it clear that he is ready to watch "the van crunching down the drive" without feeling loss or regret. This willingness marks a liberation that comes as no surprise: earlier we have seen Peter counting days left in the week as "He traced his name in spilled beer on the formica table top." Identity and time are brought together as Peter waits for his bus. Later, they are united once more when Mr. Arkle tells Jeanne why the precious grandfather clock can't be stolen: " 'It's engraved, Mrs. C. On the face, on the dial. The maker's name and date.' " The implication, of course, is that things of genuine value are connected with time and identity. By extension, people of genuine value (and craftsmen like the grandfather clock's maker) are conscious of their identity *through* time. Some may argue, as Norah Story has, that Jeanne "uses her lover's affection for her child to make him the object of suspicion while she disappears."[3] However, to reduce the story in this way is certainly to ignore its obvious emphasis on Peter's development. He is by no means duped; and at the end, he sees quite clearly that Jeanne has been planning to rob the Compton-Smythe's. Moreover, he has known all along that it is *Jeanne* who is endangered, and she knows this herself. As she says: "They've got a description. They'll be doing the rounds. . . . How long do you think I've got here?" Peter is not left holding the bag, but the "document case" that signifies the professional teaching role to which he will return.

Imagine Peter Hendricks later in life. Peter Thornton in "Girl in Gingham" appears to be a refined version of the man in "The Lady Who Sold Furniture." The two characters share many of the same problems, and face many of the same needs. The difference, of course, is that Thornton is more directly involved in the aesthetic implications emerging in "The Lady"; consequently, his story deals more concretely with the relationship between self, society, and identity. But both these novellas pointedly return, through form and narrative device, to the question of how time broadens an individual's conception of art and experience. Although "The Lady Who Sold Furniture" has received little in the way of critical commentary, "Girl in Gingham" has been discussed at length, and in great detail, by Barry Cameron in "Invention in *Girl in Gingham*." Cameron's brilliant analysis of the story makes my task considerably easier; in fact, I confess that his discussion is so thorough, and so much in line with my own views, that I have few new insights to add. Cameron does leave me room, however, to say something about "Girl in Gingham" 's place within the scheme I have been discussing, and it is probably best to begin by suggesting how the story marks another step toward the first-person fictions I will finally examine.

Thornton is, to apply a well-worn phrase, "a rounded character." His personality is complex, and we come to know it through flashback, fantasy, and the direct observation of things which take on moral and realistic weight as the story unfolds. Thornton has a history that informs his immediate perceptions; he has a well-developed critical sense which allows him to comment on society and art (he is, after all, an antique appraiser); and he has an imagination which gives form to dreams that are continually shattered. We know Peter through his own voice as it emerges in extended dialogue, and through the third-person voice which comments ironically on what Peter is saying and thinking. One of the qualities distinguishing Peter Thornton from Peter Hendricks or David is his self-consciousness, the self-reflexive impulse granted to him by a narrator who turns Peter's story into a story about art. He recognizes that the plot can easily become sentimental. Peter stops seeing Dr. Trevore because "he'd realized that his erstwhile wife, his son, and he, had been reduced to characters in a soap opera." The psychiatrist's waiting room is littered with "the stuff of comic novels, skits, the weekly fodder of stand-up comedians." Of course, Peter does live out a soap-opera fantasy as he agrees to participate in the CompuMate quest for *The love and companionship of a compatible Mate with whom we can share our deepest beliefs, our greatest sorrows, our wildest joys.* The juxtaposition of Peter's educated sensibility with the tasteless and frequently grotesque lifestyle of successive CompuMate dates invests the story with a sustained level of comedy which tends to mask Peter's tragic desperation. Following his divorce, he twice attempts suicide. And "He felt, he decided, as if he'd suffered amputation. He was no longer whole." The combination of comedy and tragedy allows "Girl in Gingham" to move in two directions simultaneously: Peter's encounters with the CompuMate women provide a fertile ground for Metcalf to satirize the debased values of contemporary society. But Peter's failure in those encounters, and Anna's sudden collapse at the end, are connected with a death of taste that Metcalf increasingly mourns.

The foregoing may give some sense of how the aesthetic components in Metcalf's initiation stories have taken on a broader meaning. Whereas David in "Early Morning Rabbits" confronts mortality as the outcome of his experience, "Girl in Gingham" is concerned with the interplay between life and death throughout. "The Tide Line" commented implicitly on the relation between writing and culture, while "Beryl" developed the comment in terms of language, literacy, and painting. "Girl in Gingham" makes the pursuit of true art inseparable from the pursuit of true love, illuminating Peter's world through the techniques outlined in "Keys and Watercress." "Girl in Gingham" is filled with the "*proper* name" of things (Peter is revealed by his knowledge of "Luristan Bronze Age artifacts, Solingen sword blades, Delftware"). Time is connected with the ability to "write it down" (Peter composes a five-page letter to Anna: "Looking at his watch, he saw with surprise that he'd been working on it for more than three hours"). And facts are everywhere. At Elspeth McLeod's apartment, Peter notices a bowl which catches "his professional eye. Flower decoration, vigorous in the Kakie-mon style. Opaque glaze. It felt right. He checked the hunting-horn mark. The Chantilly factory before 1750." The spontaneous appraisal suggests that Peter lives in history, detail, texture.

None of this, of course, says anything about Metcalf's careful selection of objects premonitional in their force, or about his deft handling of speech patterns, or about his ability to draw every character, however minor, into the fabric of the tale. To appreciate Metcalf's intricacy we must turn to Barry Cameron's observations in their entirety. Here I can only suggest the major thrust of his argument. Cameron writes that the "controlled third-person point of view" allows Metcalf the "rhetorical flexibility" he needs to explore several dialectics, the most important of which emphasize "art and life, fictional and factual truth, reality and fantasy, comedy and tragedy, and humour and pathos." All of Peter's actions and thoughts can be explained as the result of his need to "invent" people, and so "Peter persistently sees, or 'creates,' life in terms of drama, fiction, or painting." His need for invention is obviously a response to the loss he has recently experienced. Because the search for an ideal girl in gingham is part of Peter's quest for aesthetic fulfillment, he becomes increasingly pre-occupied with Art as the story develops, a pre-occupation frustrated by what Cameron calls "the absurdity of the modern technological world." It is true, as Cameron says, that Peter suffers from a "failure to remember"; the point is that his acts of inventing extend into the past as well as the future. By fabricating his life story in the letter he writes to Anna, he simultaneously creates a private history, a personal mythology which gives him a new sense of purpose and direction. This tendency to imaginatively recreate the past will become even more pronounced in Metcalf's first-person narratives, where we find speakers developing personal mythology as the *raison d'être* of their art. The difference between those narrators and Peter, however, is that Thornton is ultimately unable to separate the ideal from the real, a fact which allows Metcalf to draw the ironies he has been developing together in the story's shattering conclusion.

No one will doubt that "Girl in Gingham" ends on a note of disillusionment. But the resolution of "Gentle As Flowers Make the Stones" is not so clear cut. Metcalf leaves us wondering if the protagonist, Jim Haine, really reaches a creative, poetic climax or whether he misunderstands the aesthetic implications of his poetic acts. Certainly Haine stands on the brink of recognizing the nature of craftsmanship as it is perceived by Metcalf's first-person narrators. He is obviously devoted to the weight of words and entranced by the tensions in punctuation. He thinks of people in terms of portraits by Bonnard, Degas, and Renoir. He ridicules the gew-gaw lifestyle of Jewish middle-classers ignorant of literature and art. He scorns the "hyphenated ladies" of the Canadian Authors Association and he tries to avoid being "trapped into the literal" so that he can emancipate himself through metaphor, finding freedom through image and sound. Despite Haine's fascination with the creative process, however (witness his concentration on the breeding fish which swim in the aquarium's "lighted rectangle" in the opening scene), we sense that he may well be a failed artist who works for money ("He needed money") rather than for love of his craft (note that the first batch of fish eggs "had turned grey" and that the second batch "had simply died"). Haine is ultimately ambivalent because he straddles the line between Metcalf's true artists and those, like Peter Thornton and Peter Hendricks, who have potential to know art but lack the ability to practise it with any degree of success.

Jim Haine plants one foot firmly on the side of Metcalf's concern with the relationship between time and space, his insistence on linguistic exactitude, and his belief that all good art is essentially subversive. He is a published poet who is being evicted from his apartment because he can't afford the rent. Poetry doesn't pay. To support himself he takes on occasional book reviews, peddles drugs, performs for Jewish Ladies' groups, and translates Latin verse. Haine's apparent skill in translation is crucial, for throughout the story his attempt to render the passage from Martial with honesty and art is juxtaposed with the commercial world associated with Pevensy of the Montreal *Herald* (the newspaper building makes Haine think of technological demise, of "Charlie Chaplin swimming through the cogs"); with the *sub*culture reality of Jackie, who calls to say that " 'The desert express is in' " (note the connection between drug and desert—Haine will not find happiness there); and with the tasteless Pointe Claire house where Haine reads "to the assembled ladies." The point is clear: Haine must do all he can to assert the primacy of art. We observe his critical sense, his ability to stand back and comment on his own translation: "There was a sense of right-ness, too, in dividing the sentences of the original into stanzas." "It needed couplets. *That* was the connection." "The *ands* repetition wasn't bad, wasn't *too* obtrusive in its suggestion of the child." Even when he sits straining on the toilet in the *Herald* washroom, Haine considers the fact that "He was being too literal. Again. He needed to get further from the text. To preserve. Intact. The main line of. Intent." The rhythm here is intentionally disjointed. Metcalf is suggesting through the sound of his sentence that the poem's release is equated with evacuation, purgation. And later, as Haine "grunted enquiry" at "a word he'd written" we begin to sense that the release of the poem is also connected with the rhythm of birth. The subject matter of the translated poem is also appropriate to Haine's quest. He is working on lines adapted from "Martial. *Epigrams*. Book V. 34," in which " 'The poet commends the soul of a pet slave girl to his parents who are already in the lower world.' " The epitaph Haine is seeking would, like Metcalf's own stories, capture the subtle inter-play between life and death as it mourns for youth's passing:

Gentle as flowers make the stones
That comfort Liza's tender bones.
Earth, lie lightly on her, who,
Living, scarcely burdened you.

The poem is exquisite, and its temporal and spatial motifs remind us, inescapably, of Haine's own poetic intentions. He is, after all, the author of *The Distance Travelled* (the title of which emphasizes his concern with time and space) and he has written several poems to be included in a new collection called *Marriage Suite*. Like the epitaph (in which earth, a lover, lies on Liza) Haine's books announce their author's concern with union, permanence, and change. When Haine mourns for Liza in the moment of conception ("Tears were welling in his half-shut eyes" as he finished "the poem perfect") he is also mourning for himself in three ways. First, he laments the artist's separation from his creation in much the same way as a mother often mourns the birth of her child. In another sense, Haine has been sexually involved with Liza, although Midge believes that the orgasm he experiences on the "summit" of Mount Royal is the result of her stimulation. When he parts from Liza, from the poem, he experiences the classical sorrow after intercourse — both in physical and aesthetic terms. Finally, he cries because he has failed to write his own poem. The orgasm is a death. The child for whom he writes the epitaph — Liza — is adopted, Martial's offspring, not Haine's. Seen from this perspective, Haine's tears suggest that the poetic affair has not been consummated, and it is not surprising to learn that Haine "could feel the sperm getting cold, running down his side, cold on his hip."

Metcalf achieves a fine tension between the metaphors connected with birth and death, inspiration and translation, creation and mimesis. In commenting on Haine, Metcalf elucidates several theoretical positions, and one of them is this: the translation may be perfect, but it is an imitation, divorced from direct observation, and therefore removed from true art. Although the epitaph contains all the elements of poetry, it is not Haine's poetry. To recognize this fact is to see Haine from the other angle I have mentioned: he is, in part, a failed artist who has "sold out" his craft. His inevitable demise is foreshadowed early when he watches the commas of fish eggs (obvious signs of writing) "drifting towards the suction of the filter's mouth." Moreover, Haine is willing to sell "all his pretty ones" to "Ideal Import Aquariums." There is even the suggestion that Haine doesn't write well. Pevensy doesn't want to review *The Distance Travelled ("Lack of space, old boy. Hands were tied")*, and he hides from Haine when the poet comes searching for review assignments. The verse he gives to Jackie is plagiarized, comprised of *Howl* chopped "into tiny sections." The material he reads from "his first Ryerson chapbook" is also unoriginal: "his Dylan orotundities," "His Auden atrocities," forty minutes of "Nature, Time and Love." All for twenty-five dollars. Metcalf may be commenting, through Haine, on the way artists are forced to prostitute themselves for money that they can't earn from book sales in a country where people don't read. But the fact remains that because Haine does not give us his own poetry (although Metcalf certainly gives us *his*) he is severed from the aesthetic act. We must read Metcalf's first-person narratives before we find a character who is ready to provide us with his own writing and its simultaneous assessment. Or as T. D. Moore says in "Private Parts":

> How neatly the rhetoric of that confession is managed! How prettily worked its repetitions, its movements in and out of italic.
> Lies. Mainly lies.

III

Moore's words isolate several of the aesthetic features that become most prominent in Metcalf's first-person narratives about writers who, in the process of creating fiction, comment on the process through which their powerful fictions are made. In its highest form, fiction becomes a mode of private confession developed from a self-conscious narrative stance; and the confession encompasses not only personal memory, but the rhetorical existence of the speaker as well. Self is revealed through aesthetic disclosure; aesthetic observation reflects a heightened concentration on the elements of narrative voice. The lying life is explored to the core of its poetics, to the theoretical heart of characters who live in art. In "The Years in Exile" Metcalf articulates his poetic through the consciousness of a senescent writer whose present circumstances in Canada are juxtaposed with his memories of a youth spent in England. The repeated shifts from observation to recollection allow Metcalf to show how immediate perception flowers under pressure from the past. But to see the story only as a set of contrasts between reverie and the direct apprehension of "Particular life" is surely to miss the point Metcalf makes about the artist's consciousness of time's geography: for the

"I" of "The Years in Exile," present is infused with past, and the body which feels this moment *is* part of the landscape it touched long ago:

> I know that I am lost in silence hours on end dwelling on another time now more real to me than this chair, more real than the sunshine filtering through the fawn and green of the willow tree.

The immediate world can only be explained through its relation to remembrance, to the pictures formed in the mind of one who believes (by way of reading, and often parodying, Joyce Cary's *To Be a Pilgrim*) that "This place is so doused in memory that only to breathe makes me dream like an opium eater." Metcalf's writer is a pilgrim ("Yes, I have thought myself a pilgrim") and as we watch him making pictures of his life we realize that he is illustrating his own voyage from the Old World to the New. His Old World, of course, encompasses the magic of Fortnell House, a dilapidated English mansion containing "letters, newspapers, parchment deeds with red seals, account books, admiralty charts and municipal records"—a veritable museum displaying the writer's own concern with heritage, artifact, lineage, language. It is no coincidence that the owner of the place—Sir Charles—"had devoted his energies to Christchurch and the county collecting local records, books, memorabilia and the evidence of the prehistoric past." Fortnell contains "shelf after shelf of books," books which the speaker refers to as "my milestones." The New World is Canada, but it offers little in the way of hope. In this land lacking in tradition, the writer is a permanent exile. "I have lived in Canada for sixty-one years covered now with honour yet in my reveries the last half century fades, the books, the marriages, the children, and the friends. I find myself dwelling more and more on my childhood years in England...." The English landscape bears witness to history, birth, and death. But in Canada time is frozen, or refrigerated like the writer's manuscripts, which, he surmises, "will be consigned to some air-conditioned...oblivion." Obviously there is a powerful contrast between the papers at Fortnell House, covered with mould, dampness, evidence of change, and the writer's papers, which are to be put "in order" and preserved. Similarly, there is a distinction to be made between the man "cataloguing the library at Fortnell House" (a man clearly involved with tradition) and the "young men with tape-recorders and notebooks" who come to interview the writer in his age. The young men, we learn, are "difficult to talk to" because their "minds no longer move in pictures." Implicitly, the writer *has* been able to communicate, to find art because "My mind is full of pictures."

He illustrates the picturing-reading-writing relationship in several ways. For example, he remembers his grandfather by creating a vignette of him "conducting barely audible arguments in two voices, dozing, his crossed leg constantly jiggling, the dottle from his dead pipe falling down his cardigan front." Note that the picture says as much about its creator as it does about the subject: the grandfather is involved with *voice,* as is the writer himself, and the description is self-consciously literary and alliterative, with its repeated "d's" and "c's." Moreover, the picture, which draws our attention to "dozing," "jiggling," "dottle," and "falling" conveys the writer's own fear of senility and death, his own awareness of an impending fall which might fill him, or make him unable to hear, or make his muscles jiggle. The technique of using visual images to convey the relationship between style and consciousness is paramount throughout the story and evident from the start. Take the first paragraph:

> Although it is comfortable, I do not like this chair. I do not like its aluminum and plastic. The aluminum corrodes leaving a roughness on the arms and legs like white rust or fungus. I liked the chairs stacked in the summer house when I was ten, deck-chairs made of striped canvas and wood. But I am an old man; I am allowed to be crotchety.

The striking feature of the language here is its sparseness, a sparseness which denotes Metcalf's own determination to sharpen his prose by eliminating adjectives and concentrating on the particular details which define felt life. The speaker pictures his own condition by concentrating on the chair which situates him in a contemporary world of "aluminum and plastic." In characteristic fashion, the second sentence modifies the first by suggesting that even the aluminum and plastic are subject to change imaged through corrosion, "white rust or fungus." We are being subtly introduced to the story's temporal contrasts, and by the third sentence, we know that the contrast will involve a juxtaposition between present and past: the "deck-chairs made of striped canvas and wood" stand against the "aluminum and plastic" present, and are concretely linked to visions of youth and summer. By the end of the paragraph, the speaker tells us what we have already inferred: "But I am an old man." The important part of that statement is not the admission of age; it is the word "But." As the second and third paragraphs unfold, we see this word repeated two more times. The emphasis suggests an initial impulse to suppress any form of critical expression: "But I must not get excited"; "But I should not complain." Yet in his very assertion of the need to remain calm and complacent, the speaker tells us that he can never remain that way.

The first word of the story—"Although"—prepares us for the voice of a man who will take exception to something, and in the course of reading the first page we discover that he takes exception to every sign of modernity: Adidas running shoes ("one of this year's fads"), the "so-called college" his grandson attends, the "voice of the vacuum cleaner" heard throughout the land, the "hum and shudder of the fridge." The transition from observation to remembrance (triggered by the speaker's thoughts about his manuscripts) is so subtle that we might easily miss the correspondence Metcalf immediately establishes between memory and art. The first paragraph, which contains remembered images, is poetic in thrust: it evokes the metaphoric through the temporal image of "striped canvas and wood." But the second, third, and fourth paragraphs, involved as they are with observations on contemporary life, are devoid of metaphoric impulse. Only when the speaker turns his gaze towards "the weeping-willow tree in the next-door garden" does metaphor surface again. Significantly, the "reveries" which now begin to involve the speaker originate in the vision of *weeping* tree and *next-door* garden. Implicit in what he sees is the idea of lamentation (the tone of the story is undeniably elegiac) and separation from pastoral consciousness linked to a garden which the speaker does not own. Faced with the garden's loss, the speaker turns increasingly to pictures which he hopes will invest the present with meaning culled from the past. The "insistence of the pictures," however, is not always benign. We have seen how in remembering his grandfather the writer projects his own decay, and now we note that his vision of the "bone-handled clasp-knife" his father used is connected with a "wooden box" that might be a miniature coffin. Certainly the picture has broadened to include several graves. Note that the images of burial, death, and decay are all tied to the written word and then again to the speaker's own admission that "I will not write again."

83

He "read once" about the Dogan African tribe whose "masks and carvings are a part of their burial rites; the carvings offer a fixed abode for spirits liberated by death." This reading says a good deal about the narrator: in carving out his story he has paradoxically created his own burial rite and announced his desire for the freedom promised by death. Paradoxically again, he cannot escape the "masks" which symbolize the fictional personae he has assumed over time. Death therefore signifies not only a return to home, but return to the life-forms of remembrance liberated through fiction. Life, time, remembrance, and art are all connected in one flowing stream. The object is to find the river and follow it back to its source. So the speaker looks at his wrist and stares at the "blue veins" which are soon transformed: "The left side of the wrist might be the river Avon and its estuary, the right side the sea." Following his wrist, his body, and the metaphor of temporal flow, the narrator soon finds himself immersed in remembrance and evidence of his youth.

Because the fictionalized past has become so present, Metcalf divides the narrative here. The second part of the story is filled with temporal images aligned with the writer's dreams. Connected to his own veins is the "wrist of land" across which The Dykes of "2000 years ago" pass to meet "the estuary on the other side." The Dykes, he explains, are symbols of history, for they "were Iron Age earthworks...built presumably by the people whose barrows still rose above the turf." Although The Dykes "were eroded now by time and rabbits" the narrator still sees them on the ground upon which his dreams, stories, are built. So he connects those ancient constructs with both imaginative and physical sustenance. He would "sit beside the larger of the two burial mounds" on "the height of the land" near The Dykes to "eat my sandwiches" and imagine stories of other travellers who also lived in the past: "...for me, Hengistbury Head was Hengist's fort and I imagined inside the larger mound the war-leader's hugh skeleton lying with the accoutrements.... I gave alliterative names to his weapons." Here the act of poetic naming finds its genesis in visions of the grave, a fact which comments on the speaker's own creative dreams of death as home. That the imagined grave of Hengist links the ability to write with the need to remember is also suggested by the potency associated with Hengist. In the narrator's mind his name means "stallion"—eminent symbol of fertility—and sitting by Hengist's "burial mound" he looks out at "a narrow run of water" containing the "salmon run"—again the symbol of fecundity cannot be ignored. And all of these images are pointedly linked to the fictional process—the process of inventing worlds—when the narrator remembers "the maps I used to draw" near "the burial mounds and Dykes, the wood, the estuary and the salmon run." Closing the section, he stresses once again that these memories of birth, death, river flow, and mapmaking are present to him now. Indeed, they define him and the act of naming in which, as a writer, he has been involved throughout his life: "I can see those childish maps now as clearly as I see the petunias by my chair or the willow in the next-door garden" (note that the willow is now *in* him, and that it is no longer described as "weeping"), "I can remember the names I gave to various areas."

The richness of this section does not stop here, for in reliving his past, the narrator simultaneously re-experiences the stories he has told. "The Years in Exile" contains allusions to some of Metcalf's fiction which I have already treated as initiation tales. The "hollowed bodies of birds" which the speaker remembers finding among "sea-wrack, the tangles and heaps of seaweed, kelp, and bladderwrack" recall the dead bird found in "The Tide Line." And compare the descriptions of sea life which the writer and Charles find. In "The Years in Exile" we are presented with "Razor shells. The white shield of cuttlefish, whelks' egg cases like coarse sponge, mermaids' purses." In "The Tide Line," Charles sees "razor-shells..., clusters of whelk eggs, the white shields of cuttlefish, mermaids' purses." In fact, the writer also recalls the landscape explored by Charles in "The Tide Line." "I usually rested in the shadows of the rocks," the writer tells us, while Charles "scrabbled away towards the rocks," where he "huddled into the shadows." Anyone who compares the texts will discover many more words and phrases from "The Tide Line" repeated in "The Years in Exile," and will notice that like Charles, the writer experiences sea rocks as prehistoric forms. "The Rocks. I always thought of them as a fossilized monster." Or, "dreaming of finding the imprint of some great fish," the writer recalls that "I dug, too, at the cliff face." Alluding to "Early Morning Rabbits" and its mutability theme, the writer also recalls how The Dykes were eroded by "time and rabbits." The "slow worm" which appears in "The Years in Exile" reminds us of the eel in "Early Morning Rabbits," and its colouring ("Its belly was fawn") is reminiscent of the wounded rabbit's belly colouring. I point to these similarities because they indicate not only the self-conscious style used by Metcalf's first-person narrators, but also the critical perspective which these writers share. In re-incorporating previous fictions into the process of invention they simultaneously comment on and re-interpret the meaning of what was once perceived and told.

In the third section of "The Years in Exile" we rearrive in the present. By now we can predict the turns the narrative will take. It will begin with criticism of contemporary culture and eventually retreat into the solace provided by memory. The writer thinks of Robert with his modern "weed-killer and trowel," commenting that Robert does not even know his wooden basket "is called a 'trug.'" When he says "I hug the word" trug "to myself" (the rhyme is important) we know that he has begun the movement into art, a movement into another time when people did know what trug meant. This movement involves him directly with poetic experience, evidenced by his mention of Wordsworth: "I have always disliked Wordsworth. . . . he could not do justice to the truth; no philosophical cast of mind can do justice to particularity. I am uncomfortable with abstractions, his *or* mine." The word *"or"* is significant because it suggests that this writer might well be involving himself in precisely the philosophical and abstract cast that he claims to dislike. Clearly his narrative does not only render ideas through attention to "Particular life": it explores the abstract implications of art; it deals with complex notions of self, time, and space; it poses metaphysical problems about the nature of reality and imaginative truth. That the comment on Wordsworth is to be seen ironically is also suggested by the fact that, much like Wordsworth in "Tintern Abbey," Metcalf's writer also revisits the past and by doing so makes it present. Allusions to Wordsworth abound, as well as references to Browning and Virgil, aligning "The Years in Exile" not only with philosophical introspection but also with literary retrospection. Metcalf's writer reminds us that he cannot escape abstraction and poetic tradition; abstraction and tradition make his voice.

"The Years in Exile" contains three more sections, each of which continues to explore the nature of creative process and the apoetic values inherent in contemporary life. The narrator's self-conscious stance does not diminish; in fact, the more he recollects, the more analysis he tends to devote to his own art. "Children are, I think, drawn to death and dying," he says. The comment may be applied to "Early Morning Rabbits" and "The Tide Line," but in this instance it makes the speaker think that he once attempted a story on "The daughter of a friend" but that "as with so many of my stories, I could find no adequate structure." In "The Years in Exile," however, Metcalf indisputably *has* found the structure which allows him to superimpose tense and place in the creation of a sophisticated moving picture of the story-telling mind. Readers who want a convenient "resolution" will be disappointed: the story ends, as it began, with the writer sitting illuminated "in the sunshine," waiting to remember.

"The Teeth of My Father" is less complicated in structure than "The Years in Exile," but the story's comparative accessibility does not stop it from being one of Metcalf's most powerful—and poignant—works. The story's controlling form originates in the elegiac impulse which prompts the narrator, "in the cold fall evening of another country," to shed "scalding" tears in memory of his father buried ten years past in England. As in "The Years in Exile," this narrator—who is also a writer—finds the past more immediate than the present. The sustained elegy, which emerges both explicitly and implicitly through several fictions within fictions, suggests that in remembering his father's death the narrator simultaneously recollects and fictionalizes the birth of his own life as a story-teller. The father is, therefore, associated not only with history, but also with art, rhetoric, and their relation to identity. Casting himself in the role of critic, the narrator recollects and comments on a story he wrote "Many years ago," noting that the *"sample of juvenilia"* he has quoted is to be viewed as *"autobiographical either in fact or impulse."* Explicating the early story further, he notes that it is about a child engaged *"In nothing more or less than the act of defining his identity."* Then he asks: *"Through which functions does the child perform this act?"* And answers: *"Through naming, drawing, and most importantly, writing."* Like the characters in "Early Morning Rabbits" and "The Tide Line," and like the writer in "The Years in Exile," the speaker finds himself by exploring the components of art. Those components, in turn, are inextricably tied to an appreciation of the past. The act of defining identity, we learn, is inseparable from *"The Father"* who is *"in the words of the text, 'far away.'"* By adding this spatial reference, the narrator points to Metcalf's own belief that the discovery of art—of self—arises not only through knowledge of naming, drawing, and writing, but also through the ability to bridge geographic and temporal gaps. It is precisely this ability which Metcalf demonstrates throughout "The Years in

Exile." By juxtaposing previously told stories with the process of writing this story now, Metcalf establishes a fictional continuum reflecting the temporal and spatial linkages he must find in order to create art (to create himself). The juxtapositional structure also serves another function: it allows Metcalf to analyze critically what he has already written through the agency of a narrator who both creates, and comments on, what is read. For example, the narrator recalls that "I studied my father," a minister whose sermons showed him the basics of writing. "He was, unknowingly, teaching me what is now my craft." What was it that he learned? "Inside my head, I practiced the voices and inflections of his rhetoric, the rise and fall, the timing of the pause, the silence, the understated gesture, the rhetorical series of questions and their thundering denial." As these words make clear, the relationship between father and son, past and present, homily and story, is inescapably aesthetic.

When the story opens the narrator is "Adrift" with a friend on "a tide of beer," and in the "River Room" of the Lord Beaverbrook Hotel they "traded stories of our dead fathers." By implication, the story-telling trade is involved with the act of recollection, and the act, in turn, establishes a fictional river of time. In this respect the words "Adrift," "on a tide," and "River Room" are crucial. Soon the narrator will expand on the drinking/drifting parallel. He tells us that Cyril Connolly was "perceptive" to say that "drinking is a low form of creativity." And "Drinking," he adds, "also prompts my memory." So his drunkenness "unlocked the smells and textures of a receding past" and allows him to flow into creativity, to drift in time. Following the river to the origins of his craft, he admits influences (the description of his "wilful legs" he confesses, was "plagiarized from Dylan Thomas") and, through the form of his tale, he indicates that for him art *is* life. After all, the narrator's reality is comprised only of the stories he tells about stories, mirrors held up to himself.

In "Private Parts" the fictional mirrors continue to define reality. Metcalf's narrator is conscious — all too conscious — of the aesthetic implications arising from the autobiographical fragments he presents. "So much of my life is spent alone in silence creating illusions that even when I set out to tell the truth I cannot escape the professional gestures." Life, as he sees it, is "Mainly lies." In short, life in "Private Parts" is private art. So it comes as no surprise to learn that the narrator — belatedly identified as T. D. Moore — is himself a writer dedicated to mythologizing those autobiographical fragments which constitute the private parts of memory. That particular memory is one of a mother who thought that "The Flesh existed to be subdued" and that the sins of the body ("sex") and "The Sin Against the Holy Ghost were one and the same thing." Set against the Methodist-Puritan backdrop of Moore's past, the landscape can only be seen as a wasteland mirroring spiritual hell. And it comes complete with Anti-Christ figures and scarlet women: beginning with a river called Eden, an apple tree, and worms pinned to crosses, the story increasingly details the symbology of the Fall and the subsequent search for Jerusalem, "the New World," and redemptive art.

Is Metcalf moving toward allegory, as this brief description of the novella might suggest? It seems clear that in his most complex first-person narratives Metcalf does make use of the allegorical mode to broaden the implications of the narrator's tale and to draw our attention to the metaphorical aspects of his experiences. We know this character T. D. Moore in all his doubts, fantasies, and frustrations. We see him at the frame's centre, digressing on art, Masters and Johnson, and the impact upon him of seeing Bobby's "thing." Simultaneously, we see him acting out a small part in a huge, Breughel-like painting filled with action, sin, celebration, and desire. It is Metcalf's ability to fashion "Private Parts" as a particularized allegory that makes the novella so successful. And in Moore we find the qualities (or anxieties) which seem to define all of Metcalf's highly articulate first-person narrators: he is able to retrieve time and fashion life through memory sometimes verging on nostalgia; he knows the present, detests contemporary taste, and criticizes everything around him that threatens genuine creativity; he is an artist who expresses his own experiences by commenting on others' art and by seeing his own work in relation to theirs, he comments on himself; his language is sparse, direct, and chaste, yet full of innuendo, irony, and comic thrust; he knows how he is writing; and he is conscious of being involved in the narrative structure of his tale.

To examine that structure in more detail is also to discover Metcalf's extraordinary sensitivity to voice. "Private Parts" itself comprises two broad narrative parts, and these in turn encompass fifteen textual divisions (twelve in Part I and three in Part II). Part I is exclusively devoted to Moore's recollection of "The world of my parents" which was "pious, sour, and thin." Part II centres partially on the past, but it gradually enters the present as Moore comes closer to the reality of his situation, and to the realization that "the stories I write are exorcisms." Although the narrative (described ironically as "a titanic struggle fought against the backdrop of Hell") does progress temporally from recollection to present reality and spatially from England to the New World, its structure cannot simply be described in terms of a gradual unfolding. The fifteen sections in the novella all focus on incidents, thoughts, readings, and dreams which isolate Moore's consciousness at a particular point in time. These incidents are not only rendered from the viewpoint of the mature artist but also through the eyes of Moore as he once saw things. The private parts of the title are sexual, spiritual, emotional, temporal, spatial, and structural all at once. We know Moore's consciousness through time as it emerges in "Private Parts" 's fifteen fragments, and these fragments, in turn, serve to reveal Metcalf's own views on art, his own concern with modulating the narrative centre in order to grasp a character's consciousness as it alters over time.

Metcalf's ability to find a style appropriate to the narrator's projected age is apparent throughout "Private Parts." Moore begins his story by saying that he will be "Looking back now to those childhood times." The opening voice presents us with a sense of distance: here is a person who knows that he is looking back now, who knows the "spiky drawings of Edward Ardizzone" and frames his tale ("in later memory") with those "crabbed" illustrations in mind. The narrator is drawn to words which illuminate this "history of rural life," haunting "words like 'fustion' and 'coulter,' 'stoup' and 'flitch,' words redolent of another age." But listen to the way he introduces these words: he says that "I am not exactly sure" of their meanings. The admission marks a transition in the narrator's mental age. No sooner are the words recalled than the consciousness of another age intrudes and the narrator begins to speak as the boy who encountered these words once, for the first time, in all their magical foreignness. Significantly, it is *words* which allow him to depart from the present and to enter his tale. Conversely, the past is made present, interpreted, as it were, through the consciousness of a man who knows what it means to call a dairy land "Eden." On the one hand we have the child's perception: "I thought that lisle stockings, a word I'd heard Aunt Lizzie say, were somehow connected with Golden Syrup." On the other hand, the artist's perception investing child-hood experience with aesthetic significance: "It is a scene that Breughel painted." Or, "Behind the farmhouse is an apple tree in full blossom. Not a simple apple tree—an apple tree explosive in blossom, such an apple tree as Samuel Palmer saw." Note that as this first section unfolds the intrusion of the past upon the present is signalled by a gradual shift in voice. At first, Moore recalls his past by using the past tense. But when he thinks of the apple tree "behind the farmhouse" which *"is"* in full blossom we realize that the archetypal emphasis on temptation, and all that it implies about the garden, has entered the narrator's consciousness as he is telling the story. The tree is not only part of the past—it is here, before his sight now, made tangible through an act of imagination which in fact makes it more real in mind than it once was in matter. The entire section, of course, is replete with images of fecundity and decay, birth and death— antitheses which Metcalf has always emphasized in his attention to mutability and man's response to change. A brief list draws attention to the images which Metcalf uses as the foundation of his story: the "sexual memory" of Bobby's "thing"; "the bombing of the Yorkshire industrial town" during the war; "the wild and endless fells" contrasted with "thinning bracken, boulders, bare rock, and the circling hawks"; the "cathedral gloom" of the barn (anticipating a religious experience) set next to the secular catalogue of "nuts and bolts, washers, nails, screws, staples, cotterpins, fuses, spark plugs, coils of special wire" (the stylistic guts of the fiction).

At the end of the first section of "Private Parts" we are left with a central image: "I stare and stare," Moore tells us, at "Bobby's thing. It hangs down from a bush of black hair and it reaches nearly to his knee. It is as fat as my arm. His ballbag is huge like the Hereford in the dark stall." Contrast this conclusion (which clearly places Moore at a point in time when he does not yet know the word "scrotum") with the technical vocabulary that opens the second section. Moore quotes from Dr. Ethel Fawce's *Sex and the Adjusted You* to show that *"mental images"* of words arouse private emotions. It doesn't matter whether the words are sexual, as they are in Fawce's example. The point is that there are equivalencies between word, image, and emotion, equivalencies which both plague Moore and form the basis of his private art. In one respect, he is trying to get away from the images associated with a childhood in which "The suffering was total," away from *"The Book of Revelation* [which] is the source of much Noncomformist imagery," away from a "way of life" which "was like the enactment of a set of improving proverbs." In another way, however, Moore's knowledge of the proverbs, archetypes, and apocalyptic symbols gives his story its substance. He is bound to allegorize experience, no matter how he tries to deny his past. You may sense a contradiction at this point: does Moore see the past as ideal and memory as a refuge, or is his childhood world a nasty place that he would rather forget but can't? The answer, of course, is that the past is both tragic and comic, both ideal and repugnant, both liberating in its relation to allegory and enslaving in its celebration of the messages those allegories hold. This is the tension that fills "Private Parts" with paradox and allows us to see that Moore's fiction all resides in the past which he would ostensibly like to repudiate. And the more he concentrates on his past, the more we realize that the events he remembers reveal a good deal about his present life. He is still pre-occupied with "The antithesis between Spirit and Flesh" that marked his childhood. As an adolescent he was trapped into the Puritan frame of mind: "This burden of guilt and conviction of sin tortured me for years—dirtiness, death, disapproval, impurity—and eventually became the front line of the ravaged battlefield of my adolescence." Note that Moore is not only remembering but also commenting on the implications of what he remembers. Like all of Metcalf's self-conscious narrators, his critical faculty cannot be held at bay. He feels compelled to analyze his own emotions, thoughts, and language:

> (This will not do. The paragraphs flow too evenly, the sequence of statements rounds off the subject too neatly, leading too comfortably to the next asterisk and the beginning of another sequence of anecdote and reflection.
>
> To re-read these last few paragraphs nauseates me. They remind me of cute stories of children mistakenly praying 'Harold Be Thy Name,' such anecdotes as grace the pages of *Reader's Digest*.
>
> And what can you understand by my use of the word 'tortured'?
>
> Did you think I meant—'troubled'?
>
> The fault is mine. I have pictured my mother as a joyless puritan. But this is not the whole truth. The fault lies in my writing, feelings hidden behind humour, pain distanced by genteel irony. The truth is ugly and otherwise. My father was merely eccentric; my mother was mad....

The admissions prompt Moore to confess that he sought freedom from "the loveless world of chapel and grey rain" through Art. In section four we begin to get a clearer sense of the kinds of art which influence Moore. He is schooled in biblical story, in hymnody, and church music. He is versed in Charlotte Brontë, and sees her landscape as his own: "Mrs. Gaskell in her *Life of Charlotte Brontë* described among the books at Haworth 'some mad Methodist Magazines full of miracles and apparitions, and preternatural warnings, ominous dreams, and frenzied fanaticism....'" Most important, he identifies with the travelling "monologuist" who performed in Church Hall. It was this monologuist, Moore says, "who brought the certainty of art into my life." In fact, to read Moore's description of the monologuist's performance is much like reading a description of his own performance in the monologue which comprises his narration of "Private Parts": "He did different people by moving about the stage in different voices. There was a lady's voice, and a terrible, stern father's voice, and a younger man's voice." Obviously the monologuist's different voices reflect Moore's attempt to find the vocal personality of a different age. And he tells us, "...I knew from that moment on that when I was grown up I would be like him, become other people, be applauded, be magical." In the remaining sections of Part I, however, we see him in the distinctly non-magical process of growing up, a process marked by masturbation, or, as Aunt Lizzie might have it, by self-abuse. These anecdotes about "masturbation and guilt" are meant to be funny, grotesque, and pointedly realistic. In all of these areas they succeed. At the same time, Metcalf suggests that Moore's sexual awakening proceeds simultaneously with an initiation into art. As Moore develops his masturbatory techniques he finds himself becoming more conscious of language and books:

My reading had always been wide and precocious but now I read so much and secretly so late into the night that in school I was pale and lethargic and could hardly bring myself to go through the motions with bunsen-burners and balances and x and y and contour maps from which one was supposed to draw bumpy hills.

A Navarre Society edition of the *Decameron* contained pictures which caused Moore and his friends to gaze together, "transfixed with lust. The word itself, 'bodice' was only just bearable; such a word as 'nipple' was beyond endurance; the black letters on the white page blurred into an aura...." Here the word has become holy; the book is not only an object of desire but a sacred thing as well. But Moore has equated "the word" and The Word all along; his art is not only influenced by Wesleyan Bible teaching, but also by the persistent relationship he finds between books and The Book.

Several books seem to arouse in him a particular fervour (a fervour which increases as he moves through adolescence and comes closer to the narrative present). There are the "many intense pleasures given me by Evelyn Waugh"; "I devoured the work of H. G. Wells, Professor Joad, and the popular essays of Bertrand Russell"; "*Father and Son* by Edmund Gosse was a particular joy"; and *"Tono-Bungay, Sons and Lovers, The Moon and Sixpence, Wuthering Heights, The Constant Nymph"* affected him profoundly. "I read the plays of Christopher Marlowe"; "I identified strongly with Tamburlaine." Moore is not only involved in reading; in his attempt to cure the "puritan cancer" which "sat in my heart" he reaches out to painting ("I still pinned my hopes on Art"), to decadence (*Dorian Grey, The March of the Moderns*), to jazz ("To know anything of jazz in those days was like being part of an underground, a freemasonry which led to immediate trust and friendship; more accurately, it was like being an early Christian"). In cataloguing the many art forms with which he has been involved, Moore hints at some of the influences behind his own writing, which reviewers describe as "'sensitive' and 'finely-tuned explorations of loneliness and self-discovery.'" But Metcalf's method of presenting the catalogue says more about Moore: all of his dreams have been shattered. His idealized retreat into art is always confronted by a reality which says that life can't be dreamed forever, that life is ugly and dirty and unrefined. Once, Moore purchased a sketching pad, filled it with tracings he would call his own, and then "hung about the local park....The impression I gave,...was, I hoped, Byronic." The impression was far from that: no girl is attracted by his "artistic absorption and obvious sensitivity." The scene ends in deflation as Moore admits that "this scenario never did take place; even the ducks which surged to everyone else in the hope of bread learned to ignore me." Then he met Tony, fell in love with jazz, and worshipped the jazz greats of New Orleans, Memphis, Chicago. "Years later," Moore attempted to fulfill his dream of visiting New Orleans. And he made the trip, but it was predictably depressing: "I drove to New

Orleans through the increasing depression of the southern States, illusions, delusions lost each day with every human contact." The illusions and delusions surface again and again: the Rent Party which leads Moore away from *"the naked breast of a beautiful girl"* and toward the "glowing depths" which he filled with "noisy vomit"; Moore's decision to call Miss Roche—a potential prostitute —and his discovery that she was "a registered Nurse who administered colonic irrigation"; Moore's belief that sex will be romantic and the reality of the masked woman in the photo, "smiling" as the spiral animal horn penetrates her.

By the time Moore enters the second part of the story his initiation is complete. The sight of Bobby's "thing" has left him with permanent feelings of inadequacy; his masturbatory impulse has been transformed into a self-reflexive fiction; and the repressed puritan directive to *"Wash yourself"* emerges verbally in Moore's design to *watch himself* and come clean through his chief narrative form— that of the confession. "I must confess," he says in opening Part II, "that during boyhood and youth I suffered from what 'sexologists' call feelings of 'penile inadequacy.'" And during manhood he explores this inadequacy by comparing his own experiences, his own penile stature, to what he finds in *Fanny Hill* and Masters and Johnson reports. Why does Moore need to rely on other authors' descriptions to make his point? Metcalf suggests that Moore overlaps life and art to the extent that he cannot distinguish between the two. Or as he says in commenting on "a monograph by Sir Richard Burton on the nature of penises":

> I read of somewhere, or was told about, saw perhaps—or did I imagine this?—I am not being coherent.... As frequently happens with me, I find I can't distinguish between real and imagined events. A story told me or a story I've invented often becomes more real than an event I know to have occurred.

Statements such as these raise the same questions which emerged in "The Years in Exile" and "The Teeth of My Father": to what extent is art necessarily autobiographical either by fact or by impulse? How is the private past—one's most private part— transformed through memory until it becomes a new story, a new fiction that takes imaginative precedence over the original myth? Most important, can the artist ever avoid self-consciousness if his own life is perceived as metaphor? As Moore comes closer to the present (and closer to the act of writing as well) his tone becomes increasingly confessional. Soon we realize that all this attention to penises speaks equally for Moore's attachment to his pen. "Style betrays me," he says in a section which promises to digress on writing. But the section ends with the revealing statement: "I wish I had a big one." A big pen. A big penis. A big stick to wield in his dreams? "Why must disappointment all I endeavor end?" The Hopkins allusion suggests that Moore may be "Time's eunuch." His future holds no promise; his present is barren. Moore's potency lies in the past. So instead of endeavouring, he concentrates on remembering. As he points out when Gerry Waldmark comes for dinner, the two old friends

> . . . always talked about the past, things that happened twenty years and more ago, old wounds, old friends, old grievances, the two who were already dead, as though we could only be comfortable in mythology, in events upon which time had imposed some imaginable order. We seemed to live there more brightly than in our present, with more enthusiasm than we would in our imaginable future.

Is there an imaginable future? No one will doubt that Moore wants direction, wants to complete the "dream of journey" which defines his life. At the end, he does buy a navigational instrument, a "sextant" which he hides "under paper in a drawer in my room." But the instrument will not guide Moore into the future. It contains, we note, the root word of all the problems which have led Moore to create the exorcism called "Private Parts"—"sex"; the last syllable —"tant"—brings us full circle to Aunt Lizzie, Puritanism, and "The Sin Against the Holy Ghost." Nothing will change, and this is why, in the last sentence, Moore fondles the sextant and admits: "I'm not quite sure how it's supposed to work."

The temptation, of course, is to draw parallels between Metcalf's and Moore's art. Both men focus on the relations among time, place, and identity. Both writers want to strip experience bare through attention to the precise forms and linguistic details which make their narratives unique. But there is a crucial difference between the two men. Metcalf *does* know how the sextant works: for him, it is a navigational instrument as well as a metaphor of fictional direction.

Metcalf prefers the old, hand-held tools. Sextant over Sonar. Story over anti-story. "'None of your glue. None of your nails. None of your screws.'" While plots crumble and characters die, Metcalf keeps working to create "a different class of piece altogether" — readable, engaging fiction that will last.

NOTES

1 See Barry Cameron, "Invention in *Girl in Gingham*," *The Fiddlehead*, No. 114 (Summer 1977), pp. 120-29; "An Approximation of Poetry: The Short Stories of John Metcalf," *Studies in Canadian Literature*, 2 (Winter 1977), 17-35.

2 My textual references throughout this reading are to John Metcalf, "Early Morning Rabbits," in *The Lady Who Sold Furniture* (Toronto: Clarke, Irwin, 1970) [hereafter abbreviated as *Lady*]; "The Tide Line," in *Lady*; "Keys and Watercress," in *Lady*; "Beryl," in *The Teeth of My Father* (Ottawa: Oberon, 1975) [hereafter abbreviated as *Teeth*]; "The Lady Who Sold Furniture," in *Lady*; "Girl in Gingham," in *Girl in Gingham* (Ottawa: Oberon, 1978) [hereafter abbreviated as *Girl*]; "Gentle As Flowers Make the Stones," in *Teeth*; "The Years in Exile," in *Teeth*; "The Teeth of My Father," in *Teeth*; and "Private Parts: A Memoir," in *Girl*.

3 Norah Story, "Metcalf, John (1938-)," in *Supplement to the Oxford Companion to Canadian History and Literature*, ed. William Toye (Toronto: Oxford Univ. Press, 1973), p. 231.

Hugh Hood

Looking down from above

Preface

HUGH HOOD'S NOVELS AND SHORT STORIES have inspired a sizable body of commentary. Over the last decade critics have stressed Hood's concern with allegory, his conscious attempt to draw analogies between secular and sacred experience. He has been described as a writer deeply involved in allusive texturing enriched by a deep awareness of Catholic doctrine, metaphysics, and aesthetic theory. Hood's multi-layered works—and his reflections on them—invite philosophical response, a response which forms the basis of most explication I have read. That's good. Criticism must address questions of tradition, influence, and aesthetics, particularly when the author under study is so clearly responding to literary culture through style, structure, and metaphor. But to concentrate exclusively on the theoretical implications of Hood's fiction is to deny the intrinsic values—and problems—evident in his work. How would our reading alter if we did not know that Hood is (by his own estimation) a "moral realist"? How would our criticism change if we were unaware of Hood's debt to Romantic theories of imagination? The fundamental question is really this: how do we spontaneously react to Hugh Hood's art?

It may not be entirely possible to escape the critical contexts within which Hood's work has been seen, but in this essay I try to ignore those contexts. I want to examine "Looking Down From Above" as a prose poem in its own right. Certainly the story—one of twelve comprising *Around the Mountain: Scenes from Montreal Life*—deserves the same attention one would devote to a poem. The compressed linguistic patterns are rich in connotation and enigma; the structure invites imaginative response and forces us to confront our fictional expectations; the controlling consciousness raises questions about narrative design and purpose.

In responding to the story I have simply followed its sentence by sentence development, allowing myself to make connections, and to dwell on contradictions—Hood's and my own. This kind of activity obviously puts my reader at a disadvantage. Ideally the text (see Appendix) and exegesis should be read in parallel, a difficult task to perform. To simplify the process, I have organized my reading around the signposts Hood provides. "Looking Down From Above" has three sections which explore the relationship among nature, time, space, and art. The first-person narrator is a chatty, sensitive, observant man who, in looking down at the landscape, is also looking for himself. His quest prompts him to climb, to seek new heights, and as the story unfolds we watch him moving up Mount Royal in search of insight. The ascent (which is spiritual, physical, *and* aesthetic) is punctuated by human encounters which focus our attention on individuals caught in a cosmic drama. The story opens on a sloping street where the narrator meets an old woman whose appearance affects him profoundly. He changes his direction, begins to walk up the mountain, learns more about himself and his temporal views. Much of what he learns is the result of his friendship with Monsieur Bourbonnais, a character central to the story's second part. Thinking about Bourbonnais leads the narrator to comment on the history, geography, and topography of downtown Montreal. Through his memories of Bourbonnais and the old woman, he confronts his own conceptions of place as they have shifted over time. In the third section, he arrives at the top. From this vantage point he is able to synthesize the contradictory perspectives which have marked his pilgrimage. The story closes by picturing ambivalent vision as a means to truth. Hood paradoxically reverses the narrator's initial stance and refutes the ending we anticipated. By implication, he suggests that we look to the ambivalent act of reading, not to an interpretation which concludes.

I

* * *

"Looking Down From Above"[1]

*   *   *

Hood's title defines two directions unified by sight: height above, depth below, no geographic limits. So we can take the spatial metaphors and turn them any way we want—deep into darkness, underworld, wasteland—call it what you will. Simultaneously, the looking leads us upward to holy summits without shade, then further to infinity in search of light divine. The polarities (profane/sacred, worldly/other wordly) are bridged by an act of looking which becomes an act of vision. No. The rich associations latent in the title's spatial references make me *expect* a poetic landscape. This expectation is also a response to a question inherent in the title: who, after all, is up there looking down?

*   *   *

Fair weather implies heightened perception in my book.

*   *   *

The first sentence provides no evidence of holiness, but it does emphasize that the narrator's bifocal stance is metaphoric. "Fair weather" for him "implies" the "heightened perception" linked to the title's "Above," and places this view toward epiphany within the context of "my book." This book has colloquial, self-reflexive, and biblical meanings. Colloquially, the narrator defines himself as a common man using common speech; self-reflexively, he asserts that he is a writer fully conscious of the symbolism his "book" evokes; through allusion to The Book, he reminds us that here, as in Psalms, "Fair weather cometh out of the north." When the first line ends, we know that *our* looking will be guided by a speaker who loves to make connections. But the richness of the sentence also lies in its reassuring simplicity and directness. Concision carries possibility as a three-tiered paragraph unfolds.

A gradual reversal of the story's optimistic opening marks the second sentence. Set in "early June," with climate "clear," the initial frame seems positive. We expect the "heightened perception" to be benign. But the clarified atmosphere carries portents of doubt. The "intense yellow Montreal sunlight" ironically grants the "heightened perception" which allows the narrator to see that all is *not* right: the "Fair weather" he observes actually constitutes a drought. It is "hot and dry" as well as "clear" and "no clouds" mean no rain. Here the sentence splits to confirm what imagery has already suggested: after a pause, the speaker enters the scene, walking downward to the depths.

* * *

...towards the crowded fenced stinking Eaton's parking lot, construction on the road ahead, knotted clumps of honking cars to my left,...

* * *

A cacophonous fallen world. The cars are knotted; the speaker feels constrained. To his right he confronts the tomb-like "black marble and gray stone walls" of a building blocking the "sidewalk" with its shade. The final four-word sentence of the paragraph summarizes the descent theme through empirical observation: "The road sloped downwards." This flat statement serves two purposes. It counterbalances the first line's emphasis on height with a recognition of depth and gives the paragraph proportion; it establishes some basic height/depth metaphors that will be expanded, permutated, as the story finds its form. Like the three-tiered opening paragraph, the story has three parts, each of which explores the height/depth exchange, and all its implications, from high and low vantage points.

But this is looking ahead. Hood's design spreads out from the very first part of the story, a narrative division encompassing roughly three pages of text. As he moves along his sloping road (which now "gets little sun") the narrator's heightened perception of depth merges with an awareness of death. The downtown neighbourhood, he realizes, is "murderous" — strange word to describe a landscape devoid of human violence. Yet the atmosphere declares war on life, obliterating identity in a "drab," "fake," chaotic present. The street is sided by "gutted shells and piles of rubble reminiscent of Berlin in 1945." And everywhere he looks the narrator finds signs of ambiguous termination among the city's "ruins" where "unlovely unfinished apartment blocks" threaten "a dubious future." What began as a downward journey into unsafe space leads, step by step, to temporal uncertainty voiced by an increasingly anxious "I" who finds his steps becoming "reluctant."

*   *   *

The concentrated dry heat stimulated feelings of mortality and
a sense of the passage of time. I thought how this slope must
have been without concrete or asphalt...

*   *   *

He is being sloped into a scene of finitude. A fallen scene is at hand,
but no sooner is it stated than a paradisal counterforce appears. The
narrator remembers the silent pastoral setting ("when deer ran on
the mountain") on which this noisy city was built. Placed at the end
of the second paragraph, these images of innocence oppose the
corruption accompanying the downward walk and reinforce an
emerging pattern: the narrative, like its title, develops a set of implied
contrasts between nature/noise, remembrance/observation. These
contrasts originate in the primary distinction of above/below.
"Above," the speaker now suggests, is connected with innocence: the
deer's pastoral home is "on the mountain"; the pristine "silence"
began "a hundred yards *north* of the river." The most depressing
features of the city, on the other hand, are found *"south* towards
President Kennedy."

So far the binary exchanges have emerged through setting.
Though the speaker's altering emotions are reflected in all he sees, he
has yet to implicate himself directly. Now, however, the above/below
metaphors begin to affect him. He thinks about his own mortality,
his own purpose. The self-searching is prompted by an encounter
with a "small old woman" who is trudging up University Avenue.

*   *   *

Coming slowly towards me, dragging her way up University,
was a small old woman, almost dwarf; this was the first time I
ever noticed her though I often saw her afterwards.

*   *   *

The woman's stature presents us with a human version of the descent
motif. At first this dwarf-like person seems to embody all the negativ-
ity associated with the world below. She moves with "hesitant steps"

reminiscent of the narrator's own "reluctant" downward stepping. And, like him in his descent, she too is shrouded by shadow. They approach each other slowly, she from below, he from above, and the moment before crossing freezes the story in an instant of definition: "the details of her appearance were extraordinarily sharply outlined and seemed pregnant with unstated meaning." We naturally wonder what that meaning is, and the planted question propels the narrative into the last four paragraphs of its first part.

* * *

That woman am I. To her state must I come in time.

* * *

The University Avenue meeting between narrator and woman has an important setting. The street connects their crossing paths to learning, and suggests that journeying will be identified with an acquisition of enlightenment, another version of the "heightened perception" still to be found. But this special knowledge is not gained through immediate access to the above; epiphany is born from action particularized in mortal time and space. So the woman "deeply lined" with age bears the indelible marks of travels over "diggings in the roadway." Her "run-over boots" are "splayed," "worn through," and "scuffed" from so much walking. She carries the burden of "unstated meaning" which suggests that her loneliness and dilapidation are faced by all people in old age. Possessed by this recognition, the speaker experiences the insight his voyage along University has earned: "That woman am I. To her state must I come in time." Then, "labouring under a drastic perception of the human soul in her," he sees that the woman embodies not only "I" but all of us as well. Although the recognition is tied to loneliness and loss, it also offers a vision of hope. The desolate woman is indomitable, "impenetrable and indissoluble." While her steps may be hesitant, still "She came on," "She kept coming." Despite the sunken face "She was full of life"; despite her outward shabbiness "there was fury in her eyes and extraordinary purpose." The short woman is a tower of strength. Her determination to climb the slope testifies to the persistence of the human spirit.

*   *   *

At the corner I turned back and saw her standing on the top of the rise by Sherbrooke waiting for the green light.

*   *   *

By the end of the first section the old woman has moved up to "the top of the rise." There she stands, waiting for the "green light" grail, a signal of her quest. In contrast, the narrator is at the bottom of the slope looking up — at the woman, at the path he too will take in days to come. He has become an old woman looking up from below.

Above and down are superimposed. The looking process changes. First, we see panorama. Then looking narrows, focussing down on month and place. Then it narrows further: a parking lot and buildings. Details crowd the scene in this "murderous neighbourhood." But no sooner is the locale made present than it is extended in time and space. The looking process therefore moves from expansion to contraction to expansion, from deer on mountain (history) to woman on hill (here) to "the human soul" (eternity) to one downtown street (now). This oscillating movement reflects the narrator's spiritual and perceptual development. His tendency is to begin with a panoramic observation that soon takes him over, involving him so directly that he *is* the scene. However, this subjective involvement is a catalyst which encourages the speaker to expand the moment through connection. Panoramic consciousness returns, enriched by contact with the immanent. When the expansive viewpoint is employed, commonalty is stressed; the contractive stance reverses the process, directing us to "I." The central encounter in this section extends the man/woman meeting toward concrete *and* metaphoric experience.

II

*   *   *

You can't get too close, learn their names, start talking to them, or you become irrecoverably committed.

* * *

The interplay between panorama and particular makes us expect
another version of the closely studied woman. Broadening his gaze,
the narrator describes her as typifying all of "them" who struggle in
the face of implacable odds, all of "them" determined to remain
"impenetrable and indissoluble." Why *can't* you "get too close,"
"learn their names," or "start talking to them"? To get close and
learn is to "become irrecoverably committed." The counterweight-
ing here is clear: distance versus involvement, withdrawal versus
knowledge, anonymity versus identification. These pairings not only
remind us of a task confronting the narrator (how to balance
external observation with subjectivity), they also engender other
versions of the height/depth dualism governing the story's first part.
Distance from particulars grants an omnipresent view which sees
community rather than individuals; irrecoverable commitment
implies in-depth awareness, the ability to name and know. On one
hand the teller seems content to watch and dream (dream dissolves
the temporal frame, extends him into allegory); on the other, he is
compelled to grapple with the scene (scene framing place, isolating
him in time). Hood's method emerges through his handling of these
oppositions; heightened perception provokes aesthetic encounter.
The world is rendered mythopoeically (descent, ascent, search for
self: hell, heaven, quest for salvation), but simultaneously it is
presented as anti-myth (this one man walks this one street, commits
himself "irrecoverably" to now). Like the shifts from art to life, the
language also changes. Sight starting from above produces the
connotative grammar associated with the narrator's attempt to view
his book (his look) in the context of literary form; sight transferred
to below yields concrete denotation (how far can we take the "black
buttons" on the woman's coat? Not as far as the "unlovely unfinished apartment blocks" which "jut up from the ruins"). The conno-
tative/denotative transitions are easily marked; in fact, they are
marked enough to obstruct the narrative by directing us to an
intention which threatens to become didactic. Hood wants us to
know that in his view the world is numinous, that secular activities
are analogies of the sacred, universal, and eternal. So the old woman
can't just be an old woman. She must be an embodiment of "the
human soul" as well. The narrator cannot be only a man. Endowed
with heightened perception, he contemplates the nature of man's
soul.

But the didactic elements don't gain control. The remarkably even cadence of Hood's language carries us through the potential lesson. Hood is able to recognize the precise point at which tone must shift in avoidance of the heavyhanded. Listen to the deliberately simple rhythms which introduce Monsieur Bourbonnais and his wife:

> Take Monsieur and Madame Bourbonnais, what were they to me when we came to Montreal? The concierge in our apartment and her industrious husband; that was all.

It is appropriate that they appear after a glimpse of the old woman waiting for her light. Like her they are among the unknowns who give the city its character. Their tasks have been Sisyphean too. But we don't know any of this yet; the emphasis is on appearance. Madame Bourbonnais is "a terribly pretty vivid woman" who was "always working." Monsieur is "Balding, with a fringe of still black hair over his ears, with light step and great energy." We do know that the narrator's simple articulation of the name "Bourbonnais" makes him "irrecoverably committed" to their story. We also sense that this commitment will energize his own awareness, purpose, drive. After all, his first contact with the Bourbonnais finds him *above* the depth which marked his solitary downtown voyage. He lives "on Maplewood, across from the delightful woods, and the paths leading up to the University." The setting recalls the pastoral mountain vision mentioned earlier, as well as the sloped street (University Avenue) on which the narrator travelled down to the city. But now there is a difference: descent has been reversed, the mountaintop is closer, the trees are delightfully real. From this new lookout the narrator confirms the analogy which he previously inferred: heightened perception links the individual to his community by providing him with panorama. The act of climbing plots ascension into family, culture, continuity. When the speaker voyaged downward he did so alone; emphasis was on the "I" around which experienced coalesced. Then the turning glance back upward at the woman on the hill and a glimpse of the collective human soul. Higher now, closer to the top, viewpoint shifts again: rising from his isolation the speaker finally addresses *us*, draws *us* into the spiralling significance of "Above": "*You* can't get too close," "*you* become irrecoverably committed." We join the narrator, are implicated. A *family* takes shape, surrounds the narrator, influences his pronominal awareness: "*we* came to

Montreal," "*our* children," "*our* place," "*our* block," "*my* wife."
We are introduced to couples, groups, society, home, but the introduction unfolds so gradually that we hardly recognize our shifted
stance.

*   *   *

He had a lot of plumbers' and electricians' and carpenters'
equipment, and was handy with it. We got so we didn't have to
ask him to fix something, he was so obliging and so busy.

*   *   *

Everybody knows Monsieur Bourbonnais, the small, quiet, efficient
man who competently fixes everything. In "Looking Down," however, his function as *repairer* places him in contrast with the *des-
troyers* who made the downtown "ruins" and toppled buildings into
"gutted shells." The gradual accumulation of positive terms ("industrious," "beautiful," "dignified," "happy," "kind," "responsive,"
"handy," "obliging") culminates in learning (Bourbonnais "taught
me much"). What is the nature of this teaching? Clearly Monsieur
Bourbonnais' activities provide a model of devotion to family, work,
friends. In this regard he stands as an exemplum of the "impenetrable
and indissoluble" human qualities first perceived, albeit fleetingly, in
the dwarf woman. Bourbonnais embodies the "lesson" of the
woman in another way: he is weighted with the burden of human
experience symbolized by the newspaper poundage he so ardently
collects. The newspapers provide a continuing record of man's
activities through time, just as Bourbonnais' "scrapbooks of hockey
pictures" resurrect the past in a gallery of "vanished greats of *Le
Canadien.*" Bourbonnais collects time.

*   *   *

When he wasn't fixing things in his spare time, he worked on
one of his personal collections or projects. Once he showed me
his scrapbooks of hockey pictures, and we talked for two hours
down in the garage about the vanished greats of *Le Canadien*.

*   *   *

Call the collections heritage and pattern surfaces again. The more you climb the mountain the more you know your myths, your family, your culture. In one sense, *Le Canadien* epitomizes these three forces because their history forms a widely acknowledged legend of brotherhood. Their victories were ours, are ours, even today. Moving closer to the heights makes the meaning of brotherhood more specific: from *Le Canadien* we turn to the Bourbonnais brotherhood itself—the "whole family"—and find them introduced collectively in terms of their habitual voyage *north*, a geographic transmutation of "Above" which brings them to "the Laurentians," well-known region of mountains and woods. There, they often engage in what might be seen as an eminently religious activity: "Fishing." The suggestion? Even in their most daily pleasures the Bourbonnais are involved in *higher* pursuits. No wonder Monsieur Bourbonnais knows about "special places...on top of the mountain" which spread out from the giant crucifix that gives Mount Royal's summit its special Christian air. And no wonder the Bourbonnais boys are "giant big guys" whose occupations tie them to the heights. "One was a qualified optometrist." His profession identifies him with vision and reminds us of the "heightened perception" sought after in the story from its first line. The other son is at the *"Hautes Etudes"* and "doing well." Higher studies and clarified vision are means of reaching the eternal. I hesitate to say the eternal and divine because the holy dimension of the Bourbonnais' experience must be deduced; it is never stated. Yet the deduction is encouraged by every detail of their family life, by the way their secular activities assume sacred qualities.

* * *

They were great on picnics.... It was M. Bourbonnais who told me about the picnic spots on top of the mountain, back of the University. Apparently they used to go up there quite a lot; they had special places they were fond of, and their picnics used to run to four and five hours of dining and relaxing in the sunshine, in one or other of the groves and recesses in the mountain woods.

* * *

These meals so impress the narrator that he mentions them twice, and the second time, we note, he concentrates on the predominance of wine: "They went in for very elaborate picnics...apparently including a huge meal and a lot of wine." The extended mountaintop meals assume the form of pastoral feasts. The generic identification is important because the narrator will soon equate the Bourbonnais' pastoral experience with his own understanding. He too will climb the mountain to "carpets of silky, fine grass, exactly right for picnicking," he too will drink wine as his senses sharpen. The consumed wine (later joined with bread in the narrator's own mountain feast) is undeniably Eucharistic; the meal parallels the messianic banquets prepared for those to be redeemed on Mount Zion and suggests a host of biblical suppers which promise joys in the kingdom to come (anticipated in the narrator's eventual vision of "the next world").

As we follow the Bourbonnais' rituals, then, we are really being led three ways: into daily life, into archetypal experience, into religious allegory. In its redemptive framework the Bourbonnais story takes us far from the downtown inferno of the opening scene. Had the contrast remained external to the narrator we would be left only with evidence of his *literary* ability to engineer the conflicts, cleverly extending their scope. What makes the contrast special is that the narrator is possessed by what he once empirically observed. How will "I" reconcile his expansive grasp of another world with his recognition of daily forces in the here and now? How can I find the indissoluble strength evinced by the old woman and Bourbonnais? How can I rise to the point at which I am looking down from above?

The last question implies the narrator's own search for salvation. He may find grace, but first he must climb further, must heighten his perception step by upward step. And so he continues climbing into pastoral experiences which appear to be redemptive.

* * *

You could walk up through these woods and see a surprising amount of minor wildlife, rabbits, woodchucks, the occasional badger and plenty of game birds, pheasants and partridge, usually in pairs.

* * *

He pauses to consider that on the "north side of the mountain" one can find wildlife. Again, the geographic reference to "north" is paired with nature undefiled, with a movement away from the city paralleling the Bourbonnais' northern excursions in search of fish and recreation in the Laurentian Mountains. Looking upward now encompasses not only "north" but nature, garden, growth; in short, everything the city, in its southern lower reaches, threatens to destroy. Here we recognize that the north/south, nature/city lines are drawn by reader and narrator alike. As lookers he and we become increasingly aware of the difference between "above" and "down" as the tale develops.

Our awareness is primarily metaphoric, but the story's shifting spatial emphases also direct us to an increased sense of boundary in the physical world. If we look back to the opening description of the downtown area we can see that the borders there are as indeterminate as the "ambiguous images" reflected in the fake marble wall. Chaotic setting: confused speaker. Now, however, delineation emerges at every point. The narrator's precise rendering of objects and events suggests his growing certainty about place, time, grace. Now "the ground slopes sharply upwards." Direction is reversed, and he can note the difference in the property "bordering" on "the south side of Maplewood" from land on "the north side of the mountain."

*   *   *

Once my daughter planted some flowers and a little lettuce in the borders round our building.

*   *   *

Flowers and lettuce are an important part of the larger garden the narrator has been cultivating in his pastoral vision of mountain play and picnicking, in his remembrance of deer, wildlife, woods. Borders are crucial to this vision because pastoral existence is most easily recognized when it is threatened by outside forces. Take the topographic viewpoint which appears after the mention of animals, "flowers," "lettuce," and "lawns." We learn that in its building projects "the University has started to whittle away at the woods."

"Up above, though" (over the city) "there's still plenty of cover" which makes the surviving foliage a kind of haven and retreat. As the narrator's gaze travels upward he thinks about pathways to new heights.

* * *

...leading down from the high point of the north side of the mountain, is the University ski run, a short but steep practice run which is quite a test of skill.

* * *

Set in the centre of this second portion of the narrative, the ski run is a translated version of the sloping path so central to the narrator's downtown walk. How will the hill affect him this time? Although he has yet to reach the top, he no longer frames a backward glance upward. His understanding broadened through contact with the Bourbonnais, he begins to investigate more fully the implications of height. Concentrating on the "rock walls" forming mountainside ravines, he is led to comment on the "rock-spring water" produced in spring. In a broader context, however, the analysis of water movements is an inquiry after beginnings, alpha starting in spring-time from elusive mountain source.

As you get closer to that source landscape becomes purer, more pristine:

...a five-minute climb takes you into superb picnic grounds hardly touched by the University's clearances, and in the early summer a place of fantastic and unexpected beauty.

Pause here for a moment and find the narrator. Through digression and description he has brought us away from the city and part way up the mountain's face, but *physically* he has distanced himself from the action. He's down there telling us what we are seeing here, above. How does he know what we see? The question can only be answered by referring to temporal stance. The narrator has made this voyage before and can therefore act as a guide: he recollects rather than experiences. But if we accept this temporal frame, discrepancies emerge, for the story purports to trace the *process* of discovery from the viewpoint of one who has completed it. If the narrator has already assimilated the knowledge he seems to be gaining, does this not undermine the quest motif which dominates the story and suggest that the pilgrimage is contrived? If we concentrate on literal meaning the narrator certainly appears duplicitous: even when he was below he knew what it meant to be above, knew how his story would end, knew that Bourbonnais would fall ill, knew that he would reach the mountaintop. But remember that the narrator is primarily concerned with literary meaning, with the forms heightened perception will take in *his* book. In its rendition of those forms, the narrative is authentic. The speaker intentionally arranges his story as a romance in which the process of arriving at self-discovery is announced through retrospection. A twice-told tale.

Told twice, we return to the "superb picnic grounds" through "a very well-worn path." Physically, spiritually, it gets harder to go higher: "the climb is steep." It represents a test of strength and faith. We are no longer confronted by one named roadway — "the paths diverge" and present us with possibility. What is the best route to the top? What choices must be made in order to escape the depths? These are questions posed to the reader, but they must be resolved by the narrator as well.

* * *

You might even be able to get down the sheer face of the last seventy-five feet, if you knew it well. I've never tried.

* * *

He must try. But first he must reach the top. He knows that the path to take "is that leading around the edge of the rocks to their highest point," but his knowledge is not the product of a genuine struggle. He finds the top too easily, bypassing the self-examination this difficult climb should provoke. No sooner are the choices identified than we find him "At the top of this canyon or gully...looking almost straight down." The story's opening perspective turns upside down and the title seems to fit: now we do seem to be looking down from above. Because the passage from depth to height appears complete, we might expect the story to stop. The narrator's heightened perception of the human condition would have been implied. Yet it would also have lacked impact; the narrator still has not convinced us that he has earned insight, nor has he shown what his climbing has revealed. It is one thing to get us to the top; it is another to explain how we got there.

(You see that I'm beginning to lose faith in this man. The patterns are too easy. I want him to show me that he doubts; that the climb *is* steep and hazardous; that the pathway is continually obstructed; that he really has to overcome landslides, torrents; that he really has to fight his way up there. He must convince me that heightened perception is hard to find. Must show me his mistake: he hasn't reached the top. The picnic grounds are too pleasant, too easy to find. What about the old woman in her loneliness? What about the "murderous," "stinking," "crowded," "dismal" downtown neighbourhood?)

Hood (I stress emphatically his dissociation from the narrative consciousness) seems to recognize the limitations of his narrator who is, even at this point, paradoxically short-sighted in his belief that perception from the heights is the same as heightened perception. Fair weather does not always mean vision; light often shines out of darkness. If the narrator learns this he might see that his ambiguous downtown walk *was* vision. To recognize ambiguity one must know what is clear. Heightened perception is being redefined. Hood refuses to make the conventional equation between clearsightedness and epiphany; by doing so he rejects the very notion upon which his narrator founded the story. The narrator's genuine growth is not marked by his progress up the mountain so much as by his final discovery that what he once believed ("Fair weather implies heightened perception") is false. We begin with a lie and end with a realization that reverses the initial position: "good vision" does not imply "fair weather." The story's strength may now be explained in new terms. Hood's approach is ironic. His narrator is most observant when he is most confused, most clearsighted when "outlines were blurred."

Reversal. He gets to the picnic grounds and things seem good. Climate fine, insects absent, "profusions" of flowers, bread and wine, courting couples passing, slumber in the sun. But just when the salubriousness begins to strain, a counterforce appears:

> As the sun moved the colours changed and the shadow of the thick foliage began to fall across the pages of my book; when it

obscured them completely it was time to go.

A number of key ideas are contained in this casual reference to shade.
The mountain now holds both light and darkness. It houses shade,
marks time's passing, and recalls the "feelings of mortality and a
sense of the passage of time" which the narrator experienced in his
downtown walk (in shade). Naïve optimism is replaced by recognition: there *is* obscurity in height. Most important, the "pages of my
book" (the pages of the story) are obscure. The "book" here is
doubtless "my book" of the story's first line—a book which has
changed. It was originally linked to sunshine and fair weather; now it
accommodates shadow.

III

This chiaroscuro consciousness is most pronounced in the story's
third part, the culminating textual division in which the narrator
finally discovers his own makeup to be a combination of clarity and
obscurity. Why are the first three pages of this section so loosely
textured? Metaphor is strangely absent, imagery is unpronounced,
and connotation dwindles as Bourbonnais' illness is announced.

*   *   *

After a couple of years of such pleasures we moved away. I felt
sorry to say good-bye to the Bourbonnais, especially since
Monsieur had not been well during our last few months in the
building.

*   *   *

Bourbonnais still has a great deal of nervous energy. He devotes
himself to fixing the car because "I want it perfect." There might be
some correlation between damaged car and damaged life, but the
meaning of the parallel seems too obvious: all things decay, therefore
time is precious. In the broader context of the story, however, this
message is central. The narrator has been persistently confronted by
mutability. It is not only the old woman who stimulates a "sense of
the passage of time." Human appearance alters, light patterns

change, Monsieur Bourbonnais collects newspapers, buildings replace forests, and late June becomes "the autumn of summer's first pulse"; moreover, the action takes place over "a couple of years," though the impression we gain is of a single month. The disparity is interesting because it suggests the narrator's response to time: he wants to stay in June so he can save up summer. To conserve time is to preserve life. His fascination with Monsieur Bourbonnais' energetic body work is a response to the view that "we are all given a certain amount of vitality to spend, so to speak, and Monsieur Bourbonnais had been prodigal with his, spendthrift."

* * *

It made me wonder if I wasn't perhaps a little miserly with my own capital, perhaps playing things too cagily, which is certainly one of the possible errors.

* * *

This statement *cum* confession marks a turning point in the story because, for the first time, the narrator is self-critical. He tells us that he has played it safe. By implication he has played the text too cagily, hesitating to take chances or expend his energy on the most dangerous part of the narrative — the final mountain climb. He knows that the paths lead higher than the picnic grounds, yet he has consistently refused to relinquish his pastoral comforts. His refusal is explained by the paradox noted earlier: formally the narrative promises redemption in the heights, but from his twice-told perspective the speaker turns the formal expectations upside down. He sees that the higher you get, the murkier things are. Height does not release you from this world; it forces you to see its depths. Being "above" only makes you more aware of all that is below. Getting to the top therefore means accepting the unconventional ending: the ultimate vision will not be clear but confused. Revelation may encompass darkness. The test is whether one can live with the ambivalence. For the narrator this means that he will have to abandon all the neat contrasts through which he structured his looking.

Can he transcend the polarization implied in the story's title? Certainly the tone alters after the narrator senses that it's "Better to be prodigal than miserly." Now he seems more willing to synthesize antitheses. In these last few pages Hood unites all the spatial and temporal motifs which were at odds during the first two parts of the story, and produces the "strangely mixed perspective" characterizing the narrator's new sense of vision after the closing climb.

* * *

Winter went by, and most of next spring, and the last time I saw him was on Saint-Jean-Baptiste Day, late June, a big holiday.

* * *

Now the narrator's vision goes beyond summer to encompass all the seasons. "Winter" and "spring" are united in a single sentence filled with evidence of temporal awareness. Prodigally, the narrator spends time through the sentence; previously, he suspended duration, froze things into summer. But temporal stasis contradicts everything implied by the mountain. "Above" allows you to see time as dynamic, to know age and youth in flux. It also makes you realize that everything moves together, is part of panorama, the frames collapsing as you look around. Beginning and ending together, winter and spring at once, the old lady climbing the street — *there* — in the youthful tennis players whirling on their courts. Boundaries decompose.

Look at the rest of the paragraph that begins: "Winter went by...." The narrator is back to climbing. We sense that now he will find the true summit and embrace the co-existence of above and below, divinity and damnation, death and life. When we first met him, the narrator defined the weather in absolutes and referred to the sky as perfectly blue and clear. At the end of the story the atmosphere has "a qualified fineness" and what we see is "not the perfect blue sky" we knew before. Continuing his emphasis on blending oppositions, the narrator notes that "even in late June you sometimes get a day which is autumnal in tone," or, as he describes the paradox more succinctly, we observe "the autumn of summer's first pulse." The language moves us from autumn to summer in a single breath. We are no longer directed to the moment, but to the span of a year. We are no longer being asked to concentrate on a month. The paragraph begins in "Winter" and ends in "August." Time moves forward, or backward, depending on how you see it, but most important, *it moves.*

We are taken from "Winter" to "spring" to "autumn" and then back to May joined to early July which in turn becomes "mid-July" transforming itself into "August." The narrative is doubling back on itself, and as it does, we find some of its most prominent motifs displayed again, often in reversed form. The "Saint-Jean-Baptiste Day" holiday has "a solemn stillness about it" which suggests "the end of the perfect part of summer." Lovers and picnickers are celebrating, not boisterously, but calmly. Soon, calmness becomes constraint as the narrator encounters the Bourbonnais for the last time.

*   *   *

Monsieur Bourbonnais had always been thin, but now he was emaciated. He must have lost twenty to twenty-five pounds from his slight frame, and his skin looked very bad, chalky, almost colourless.

*   *   *

Time has passed. The family's traditional picnic feast is now "a strangely quiet meal" which mourns Bourbonnais' obvious illness. We cannot help but see this saddened gathering in the context of all the earlier picnics filled with relaxation and happiness. Illness is consciously superimposed on health; declension shares its force with growth. The narrator even comments on this dual perspective: "The ghost of his usual self," he says of Bourbonnais, "was haunting... this unrecognizable and dwindled body," and "In his shaky and hesitant movements I could trace the surefooted and energetic activity I was used to in him." This observation sums up many of the changes which have taken place in the speaker. Things are not so one-sided as they once were. Things combine. Distinctions are difficult to make. Nothing stands still. The narrator's words unite ending with beginning and point to the peculiar quality of his epiphany: pure transcendence is an illusion; heightened perception must be forever tied to the depths.

In keeping with this realization, the "piles of boulders, rubble and fill" originally found downtown reappear beside the ski jump in the story's last scene. The jump parallels the sloped street on which we met the speaker. We anticipate that what happens on the jump will further qualify the relation between "down" and "above," as did the University Avenue voyage. Previously, the relation emerged in contrast. Up seemed to be good, to represent pastoral existence; down seemed to be bad, corrupting, full of shade and noise. What happens to these contrasts at the top of the jump?

* * *

The view becomes staggering as you go out farther, a wide wide vision of the northern half of the city, the country beyond, and the ridge of hills, the first upthrust of the Laurentians, thirty miles north. You have the sense of the world dropping away from you.

* * *

"Vision" appears to be the product of everything we once connected with above: panorama, the north, the country, the Laurentian Mountains. But what does this "wide wide vision" show? If it illuminates 'the way,' or 'the truth,' or even provides 'an answer' all is lost, the story fails. Hood and his narrator will succeed only if they refuse the conventional ending, the *necessary* revelation supposedly brought on by height.

And they pull it off. We get to "the very edge" of the jump. Note the double meaning of "edge." Right at the top, the abyss: "You have the sense of the world dropping away from you" at the very moment you should be most secure. "The vision," we learn, "was good," a paradoxical statement considering that "the day wasn't sharply clear," that "outlines were blurred," and that "one's judgement of distance became confused." The paradox is resolved when we realize that the vision is good because it is confused; or, put another way, when you perceive the "staggering" blur you find the final vision.

Can that vision be isolated and explored? No. The narrative ultimately refuses to yield a single viewpoint which can be packaged. We do know that the last two paragraphs destroy the spatial and temporal boundaries so prominent at the start. Above might be below; eternity might be seen in a grain of sand. Watch the narrator stepping between the immediate and the eternal, death and life, after he reaches the top. He stands on the "edge" of the jump from which skiers make a "quick descent" to the "jumping off point." The moment may be life-enriching, but it's also suicidal. Blend the polarities. He looks west: twenty miles away, the "east-west runway" at the airport appears "right under my feet." Unite the compass points, fuse near and far. "In a single stride," he says, "you could step... onto the edge of the runway or into the next world." The edge of the runway: the edge of the ski jump: the edge of the next world. What has happened to above/below and heightened perception? They have been replaced by the "strangely mixed perspective" that rejects delineation.

From this mixed perspective the narrator sees that the story's characters have merged. The Bourbonnais are there, "the tennis players chased their ball," and "that old woman on University" is still waiting for her light. These are the people with whom he has identified at various points in the story. The last paragraph unites not only stages in the story but stages in life as well: it synthesizes human time and allows the narrator to be the old woman waiting for her light, to be Monsieur Bourbonnais who "wanted it perfect," to be the tennis players whirling near their ball. The overlap refers equally to space. The old woman in the downtown area meets the Bourbonnais relaxing in picnic grounds on the mountain, and she meets the tennis players, higher still. So in his final glance, the narrator looks "directly down" to see visions of height united. He is a mediator between down and above, a link between here and hereafter. You may want the final tension to produce a message, some truth applicable to Hood's canon. But why conclude when Hood's aim has been to refuse the obvious conclusions, to deny the temptation of an ending that would have dragged the narrative into predictability and didacticism? Like the teller who is left neither here nor there, the tale ends in mixture and mystery. And that is its strength. The final sentence resolves nothing and celebrates only the unknown: "Human purpose is inscrutable, but undeniable." The language is within its rights.

NOTE

[1] My references throughout this reading are to Hugh Hood, "Looking Down From Above," in *Around the Mountain: Scenes from Montreal Life* (Toronto: Peter Martin Associates, 1976).

Appendix

The text of
"Looking down from above"

FAIR WEATHER IMPLIES heightened perception in my book. Once in early June, clear, hot and dry, intense yellow Montréal sunlight topped with blue, no clouds, I came down the west side of University south of Sherbrooke towards the crowded fenced stinking Eaton's parking lot, construction on the road ahead, knotted clumps of honking cars to my left, and the unprepossessing black marble and gray stone walls of an office building leaning over the sidewalk on my right. The road sloped downward.

This is a murderous neighbourhood; the streaked, gray-stone building houses the head office of a locally held insurance company. The stone facing is drab and the fake black marble reflects ambiguous images. The sidewalk gets little sun here. Along Sherbrooke and south towards President Kennedy lie gutted shells and piles of rubble reminiscent of Berlin in 1945. Subway construction has passed this way, and unlovely unfinished apartment blocks jut up from the ruins, threatening a dubious future.

The ugliness of Eaton's held my eyes, that and the dismal push of cars towards Sainte-Catherine, making my steps reluctant though the slope urged them. The concentrated dry heat stimulated feelings of mortality and a sense of the passage of time. I thought how this slope must have been without concrete or asphalt or monolithic department store, wire fence, diggings in the roadway, when deer ran on the mountain and silence began a hundred yards north of the river.

Coming slowly towards me, dragging her way up University, was a small old woman, almost a dwarf; this was the first time I ever noticed her though I often saw her afterwards. She moved with

By permission of PMA Books.

hesitant steps, placing one foot eight inches in front of the other, and she leaned in under the wall at an angle as if deformed in some way, in the left shoulder or neck. Our approach was slow, and for some reason I examined her carefully. It was like looking at a snapshot in a dream; the details of her appearance were extraordinarily sharply outlined and seemed pregnant with unstated meaning.

She wore small old club-like, run-over boots, splayed and worn through at the outside of the foot, scuffed. Coarse pale brown cotton stockings hanging in folds on shrunken calves, a brown dress which might sometime or other have been designed for a taller and younger person, with a row of twenty little black buttons the size of peas down the front to a loose belt. There was no question of the dress fitting her. Over it, on this hot day, she wore a man's light woollen topcoat perhaps thirty years old, hanging open almost to her ankles. In her right hand she clutched a worn purse, and from the left dangled a brown paper shopping bag with some heavy object at the bottom.

She came on and I walked slower and I saw her face, sunken and without teeth, colourless, deeply lined, her hair thick and stringy under what looked like a black cotton handkerchief, the eyes very bright and protruding like small ripe olives. She mumbled to herself. She was between seventy-five and eighty, I suppose, perhaps older, and she was alone. She kept coming.

Here, I thought, is somebody who has had to renounce all human pretensions to health, beauty, sexuality, earnings and apparently even companionship. I wondered how she lived and what she ate, whether she took pleasure in her food and her life, what kept her going. We passed and our eyes met; there was fury in her eyes and extraordinary purpose. I could hear her words and felt afraid. She was full of life.

That woman am I. To her state must I come in time. I stood on the squalid street looking at her and wondering if she would speak to me, labouring under a drastic perception of the human soul in her, impenetrable and indissoluble. Then she passed slowly up the hill and I turned downwards wondering to what purpose she gave her concentration. At the corner I turned back and saw her standing on the top of the rise by Sherbrooke waiting for the green light.

You can't get too close, learn their names, start talking to them, or you become irrecoverably committed. Take Monsieur and Madame

Bourbonnais, what were they to me when we came to Montréal? The concierge in our apartment building and her industrious husband; that was all. Mme. Bourbonnais was in her mid-fifties, I guess, and a terribly pretty vivid woman. She had a beautiful head of thick wavy red hair, dyed, but dyed smartly and attractively. She used to talk to our children and teach them a word or two of French. She looked after the afternoon newspaper delivery on our block, handling delivery-boy absenteeism by the dignified and simple expedient of taking the route herself, with a little coaster wagon. She was always working, always happy and kind.

Her husband was a wiry little man about the same age. I doubt whether he ever weighed more than a hundred and twenty-five pounds. In effect, he had two full-time jobs, working a long daily shift as a shipper in a meat-packing plant way out in the east end, and as the building superintendent at our place on Maplewood, across from the delightful woods, and the paths leading up to the University. He was always responsive to pleas for assistance at nights or on the weekend, a blocked sink, some defective electric outlet. He had a lot of plumbers' and electricians' and carpenters' equipment, and was handy with it. We got so we didn't like to ask him to fix something, he was so obliging and so busy. Balding, with a fringe of still black hair over his ears, with light step and great energy, he always would come when you needed him. He used to laugh kindly about my French and taught me much.

When he wasn't fixing things in his spare time, he worked on one of his personal collections or projects. Once he showed me his scrapbooks of hockey pictures, and we talked for two hours down in the garage about the vanished greats of *Le Canadien*. Another time I asked him why he went through the garbage and collected all the newspapers and magazines. He said that he sold the magazines for a fraction of a cent a copy to second-hand dealers. The newspapers he rolled and tied in bundles of twenty-five pounds apiece, and sold them for re-pulping, twenty-five cents a bundle, a cent a pound. His workshop was usually piled high with these bundles, amounting in all to ten or twelve dollars worth. For working in the apartment building, he got his rent, light and heat free and a small wage, and some Christmas gifts.

When this man bought his first car, a new Corvair, during our stay in the building, he paid cash for it. I never saw anyone work harder for his pleasures or enjoy them more. He used to take his family for outings in the new car, leaving at seven or eight o'clock Sunday morning and coming back around eleven at night. He and Madame and their two sons would be laughing and talking excitedly; they might have done some fishing up in the Laurentians over towards Saint-Donat.

The boys were great big guys a foot taller than their father. One was a qualified optometrist with an office east on Boulevard Mont-Royal, and the other was at *Hautes Etudes Commerciales* and doing well. They were extremely polite men. Several times when my wife was unloading a week's groceries with a child under either arm — quite a trick — one or the other of the boys came and held doors and carried cartons and otherwise helped her out. The whole family were immensely dignified, respectful of each other and of other people, without being in any way oppressed by convention. They had a free, independent life together.

They were great on picnics, things like that, which they could enjoy together. It was M. Bourbonnais who told me about the picnic spots on top of the mountain, back of the University. Apparently they used to go up there quite a lot; they had special places they were fond of, and their picnics used to run to four and five hours of dining and relaxing in the sunshine, in one or other of the groves and recesses in the mountain woods.

For many years, the University property bordering on the south side of Maplewood was pretty heavily wooded all the way from Louis-Colin to Bellingham, half to three-quarters of a mile. From Maplewood the ground slopes sharply upwards; it's really the north side of the mountain. You could walk up through these woods and see a surprising amount of minor wildlife, rabbits, woodchucks, the occasional badger and plenty of game birds, pheasants and partridge, usually in pairs. Once my daughter planted some flowers and a little lettuce in the borders round our building. When the lettuce came up, rabbits from across the street ate it. I know this for a fact because I came home late one summer night and saw one of them back on his haunches on the lawn, getting into the lettuce with his forepaws. When I stopped to look at him, he took off across Maplewood and into the brush at about fifty miles per hour.

For one building project or another, the University has started to whittle away at the woods, and in five years there likely won't be anything left along the street. Up above though, especially towards Bellingham, there's still plenty of cover. There, leading down from the high point of the north side of the mountain, is the University ski run, a short but steep practice run which is quite a test of skill. There's a tow and a jump, and a downhill run beside the jump. At the bottom of the run are soccer and football fields, and the new hockey and football stadium, an ingenious and beautiful building. West and south from here are the tennis courts, set economically and sensibly into the side of the mountain, among rocky cliffs which form neither a canyon nor a gully but something in between. The steepest drop from those rock walls might be a sheer seventy-five feet, enough to give you quite a jar. All through the springtime into June, these rocks are washed by icy water coming down from the mountainside. I'm not sure that this is just melting snow. I tasted it once and it seemed like rock-spring water to me, with a bracing mineral tang to it, very very cold.

From this sporting area, a five-minute climb takes you into a superb picnic grounds hardly touched by the University's clearances, and in the early summer a place of fantastic and unexpected beauty. You approach it from the west side of the tennis courts, where a very well-worn path leads up around the rocky cliffs through fairly heavy foliage and undergrowth, not forest but very pretty woods. The cliffs are on your left, the climb is steep, the paths diverge but the one to take is that leading around the edge of the rocks to their highest point. There is no abrupt drop here; you could climb around on the rocks if you wanted to. Lots of students and neighbourhood children do so. You might even be able to get down the sheer face of the last seventy-five feet, if you knew it well. I've never tried.

At the top of this canyon or gully (there should be a middle-sized word), you are maybe two hundred feet above the tennis courts, looking almost straight down on them. Here the woods open out a little and there are small carpets of silky, fine grass, exactly right for picnicking, mildly warm and dry, uninfested by insects, surrounded in the early summer by profusions of trilliums and other wildflowers. After Monsieur Bourbonnais directed me to this spot, I used to spend many summer afternoons alone up there. I'd bring a loaf of French bread, some cheese, a bottle of the RAQ red Burgundy and a book, and spend the afternoon half asleep in the sun. On very clear still days, you could hear the individual words of the tennis players two hundred feet below, and sometimes a dreamily courting couple would stroll obliviously past. One such pair once fell over me before any of us were aware of each other, I full of Burgundy and sun, the boy and girl full of love.

'*Je regrette, Monsieur.*'

'*Je vous en prie, Mademoiselle, Monsieur.*'

We all laughed immoderately at the incident, then after begging my pardon again they disappeared along a path leading up past the ski jump to the very top of the mountain, another three to four hundred feet. As the sun moved the colours changed and the shadow of the thick foliage began to fall across the pages of my book; when it obscured them completely it was time to go.

On Saturdays I often found *les Bourbonnais* there. Monsieur and Madame, their sons, and two lovely girls, friends of the boys. They went in for very elaborate picnics lasting a long time and apparently including a huge meal and a lot of wine. When we met, they would always press a glass on me and a slice of cold chicken, with much exchange of formal politenesses on each side.

'*A votre santé, Monsieur.*'

'*Salut, Mesdames, salut, Messieurs.*'

'*Encore un coup?*'

'*Ah oui, merci infiniment.*'

After a couple of years of such pleasures we moved away. I felt sorry to say good-bye to the Bourbonnais, especially since Monsieur had not been well during our last few months in the building. He began to stay home from work, at first a day at a time, then for longer periods. There didn't seem to be anything visibly wrong with him, and I was reluctant to ask him about it. It was very unlike him to miss work, and at that when he stayed home he kept busy around the garage.

'I was there twenty-three years,' he said to me one day when I got out of my car.

'You're still there, aren't you?'

'Yes, I'll be back soon. I meant twenty-three years till now.' He kept his hands busy tying bundles in string and his eyes moved uncertainly. He seemed bewildered by what was happening to him.

'What do you do in the packing plant?'

'I'm a shipper. The man that owns this building is my boss. I load sacks of bone-meal, hundred pounds a sack. I often do that all day.'

'Sounds like heavy work.'

'It's heavy, you bet. I'm there twenty-three years and now I'm making a little over fifty a week. Fifty-two, fifty-three, take-home pay. It's not too much.'

'No.'

'No. I never missed any time before, couldn't afford it you know, with the boys in school. Now I find I'm nervous a lot.'

'You don't look nervous.' He certainly had no neurotic characteristics of any kind.

'The doctor says it's my blood-pressure, but he's not sure. It's hard, you know. He says, "Take some time off." But a man like me loses money if he takes time off; that makes things worse. Now the boys are grown-up it should be easier for us, and now this.'

'Why don't you just relax and sit in a chair, instead of working around in here?'

'I can't do it. I don't know why.'

He finished the parcel he was tying, put it aside and drew me after him towards the end of the garage where his car was parked. From some dark recess in the wall, he pulled out a bag of body-worker's tools, some ball-headed hammers, tubes of filler and so on, and pointed out a dent in his right rear fender about the size of somebody's headlight.

'That's the first one. I don't count scratches. Somebody hit me in the parking lot, and he don't say a word.'

'They don't know how to park, these guys,' I said with a good deal of bitterness. 'When they try to angle park, they hit you with the left front, isn't that it?'

He lay down under the car and began to tap softly on the body metal with a light hammer, using a rhythmic drummer's stroke. 'I think I can get it out,' he said, 'I don't want to put a hole in her, on account of the salt. I got to finish it today.'

'Why?'

He stopped hammering and put his head out from under. 'I worry about it all the time, but I can make it like new. You'll see.'

The next night when I came in he was finishing the repaint, and it matched perfectly; you'd never have guessed the dent was there. He was just blending in the repaint patch with the rest of the fender when I parked and came over to see how it looked.

'Like new,' I said.

'It's better than new. I took her right down to the bare metal, sized it, rust-proofed her and gave it five, six, coats. Better finish than the rest of the body. When I get some wax on, she'll be perfect.'

'I guess that's what you were after, eh?'

He stopped his smooth deft brush-stroke to turn and stare at me. 'I want it perfect,' he said. Under the glare of the bare light-bulb hooked to the overhead beam, his face looked leaner than ever.

I said, 'I hope you get what you want.'

Then we moved away and I didn't see much more of the Bourbon-nais, though I used to see their car parked outside the building on my way home from work, always looking like it had just been polished. Once or twice I happened to see Madame Bourbonnais walking through the district with her coaster wagon and a pile of evening papers, and then we'd chat about our kids or about her husband, who wasn't making too much progress. They still couldn't pinpoint his illness. It seemed to me to be a case of a great endowment of vitality in danger of being expended too fast, too early in life. I don't offer this as a medical diagnosis; but it often seems to me that we are all given a certain amount of vitality to spend, so to speak, and Monsieur Bourbonnais had been prodigal with his, spendthrift. It made me wonder if I wasn't perhaps a little miserly with my own capital, perhaps playing things too cagily, which is certainly one of the possible errors.

Better to be prodigal than miserly; it's the generous fault. Mon-sieur Bourbonnais knew how to live, and if he gave too much and spent what he had too profusely, there was magnanimity, in the exact sense, in the gesture. And at that he was economical where necessary, so that he was enabled to spend freely. He was a damned good man.

Winter went by, and most of the next spring, and the last time I saw him was on Saint-Jean-Baptiste Day, late June, a big holiday. Even though I suspected that the top of the mountain would be full of knowing holidayers, I decided to put in an afternoon climbing around the woods for exercise, for the pleasure of the view and the sense of the weather, which had a qualified fineness that day, not the perfect blue sky, and yet not misty and hazy. Summer is short in Montréal, and even in late June you sometimes get a day which is autumnal in tone, where the colour of the sky seems to bring out soft browns and dark reds from the crowded trunks and branches in the woods. You might call it the autumn of summer's first pulse, because there is a distinct break in our summer; a few weeks from May to early July are capable of almost tropical perfection, rich greens, right in the center of the palette, and exact blues. But later on, as you get down past mid-July, the grass and foliage start to go yellow, the sky is less and less often that glorious spring-like blue; you can get a lot of rain in August.

This particular holiday was full of presagings of the end of the perfect part of summer, the first rush of wonderful weather; there was a solemn stillness about it, and there weren't quite as many merry-makers up there as I'd feared. It was very pleasurable to slide along the narrow paths, quiet as some Indian might have been hundreds of years ago. The foliage was at its thickest and most lush, the air still and warm, lovers and picnickers content to celebrate calmly.

Suddenly I came out into a little clearing at the edge of the rocks, one of my favourite places, and there were the Bourbonnais, the whole family including the two lovely girls, having a strangely quiet meal. The reason for their constraint was immediately clear. Monsieur Bourbonnais had always been thin, but now he was emaciated. He must have lost twenty to twenty-five pounds from his slight frame, and his skin looked very bad, chalky, almost colourless. When I came into the clearing, he struggled to his feet and greeted me. It was strange to observe the ghost of his usual self haunting, as it were, this unrecognizable and dwindled body. In his shaky and hesitant movements, I could trace the sure-footed and energetic activity I was used to in him. He smiled slowly and proposed that I join him in a glass of wine.

I said, '*Il me plairait, Monsieur*,' and drank with him. He coughed. His family stood sadly watching us, then they began to talk with great animation, especially Madame. I nodded and smiled at her, and answered one or two inquiries about the children; then I inclined my head questioningly towards her husband.

'He's gone back to work,' she said, 'he wanted to.' Her eyes were very bright and she opened and shut them twice. Sunlight shone on her bright head.

'I'm going for a climb,' I told them, and they all wished me a pleasant holiday, and then I continued along the path towards the piles of boulders, rubble and fill, along the side of the ski jump. Then I climbed some more till I was on the approach to the jump itself, right at the top, above lovers and picnickers. I sauntered out towards the very edge. The approach rises and the sides of the artificially constructed mound fall sharply away on either side. The view becomes staggering as you go out farther, a wide wide vision of the northern half of the city, the country beyond, and the ridge of hills, the first upthrust of the Laurentians, thirty miles north. You have the sense of the world dropping away from you.

The day wasn't sharply clear; outlines were blurred, and one's judgment of distance became confused, although the vision was good. Standing on the edge, right where a skier would push off for the quick descent to the jumping-off point, I could see the main east-west runway at Dorval twenty miles away to the west, as though it were right under my feet. It looked from where I stood as if you could step in a single stride onto the edge of the runway, or into the next world.

I could look directly down on the Bourbonnais, still soberly picnicking, and below them again on girlish tennis players whirling short skirts, a strangely mixed perspective, but I couldn't hear any voices. That old woman on University had climbed and stood waiting for her green light; the tennis players chased their ball; and Monsieur Bourbonnais wanted it perfect. They were all within their rights. Human purpose is inscrutable, but undeniable.